His words were as emotionless as his expression and Bianca couldn't deny a twist of pain as their coldness washed over her.

But what else had she expected? Joy? Excitement? Surely she hadn't anticipated Xanthos would behave in the way would-be fathers were supposed to behave. *Get real, Bianca.*

"You're not suggesting I *planned* this, are you?"

"I have no idea," he drawled, dark eyebrows shooting upward. "Did you?"

"Please don't insult me!"

He nodded, as if her anger and indignation were in some way reassuring. His gaze rested upon her face. "What do you intend to do?"

"I'm k-keeping my baby, of course!"

"Good."

The word took the wind right out of her sails and she blinked at him in confusion, before reminding herself that she didn't need his approval. But that didn't prevent the sliver of hope that shot through her, like sunlight breaking through a dark cloud. "I know you never intended to be a father—"

"No, you're right. I didn't." His words effectively killed off that brief flash of optimism. "So what do you want from me, Bianca?"

Sharon Kendrick once won a national writing competition by describing her ideal date: being flown to an exotic island by a gorgeous and powerful man. Little did she realize that she'd just wandered into her dream job! Today she writes for Harlequin, and her books feature often stubborn but always to-die-for heroes and the women who bring them to their knees. She believes that the best books are those you never want to end. Just like life...

Books by Sharon Kendrick

Harlequin Presents

Cinderella in the Sicilian's World
The Sheikh's Royal Announcement
Cinderella's Christmas Secret
One Night Before the Royal Wedding
Secrets of Cinderella's Awakening
Confessions of His Christmas Housekeeper

Jet-Set Billionaires

Penniless and Pregnant in Paradise

Passionately Ever After...

Stolen Nights with the King

Visit the Author Profile page
at Harlequin.com for more titles.

Sharon Kendrick

—

HER CHRISTMAS BABY CONFESSION

HARLEQUIN

PRESENTS

HARLEQUIN®
PRESENTS™

Recycling programs for this product may not exist in your area.

ISBN-13: 978-1-335-58386-4

Her Christmas Baby Confession

Harlequin Enterprises ULC
22 Adelaide St. West, 41st Floor
Toronto, Ontario M5H 4E3, Canada
www.Harlequin.com

Printed in U.S.A.

HER CHRISTMAS BABY CONFESSION

For the ace pilot Captain Matt Lindley and his (equally ace!) copilot Paul Newrick. They vividly brought to life the world of planes, emergency landings, quick thinking and plenty of adrenaline—and their help was invaluable. Thank you.

CHAPTER ONE

THE WEDDING WAS over and Bianca was glad.

Even though all the guests had proclaimed it to be *'the most wonderful wedding in the history of the world'*.

It had been a jaw-droppingly photogenic occasion.

A Christmas wedding in a golden palace.

A handsome king marrying an ordinary woman and making her his queen.

What was not to like?

Bianca stared across the elaborate palace entrance hall. She hadn't liked being a bridesmaid for a start, even though the bride was her sister. And she hadn't particularly liked being back in Monterosso—the wealthy mountain kingdom where she'd spent many of her childhood holidays.

The marriage had taken place two days before Christmas and the great cathedral had been decorated to reflect the holiday. Swathes of holly and ivy had hung from the mighty pillars and, as Bianca had squeezed herself into her crimson bridesmaid's dress, she had tried to absorb the joy of the occasion and reflect some of it back.

But all sorts of unsisterly thoughts had started flooding into her mind as she'd followed the vision of shimmering white up the wide aisle, even though she loved her sister from the bottom of her heart and was happy Rosie had found the man of her dreams. Yet Bianca kept thinking that *she* was the older sister. That *she* was still unmarried and, given her history of love and relationships, that situation showed no signs of changing.

She probably could have dealt with the growing awareness that her life wasn't going exactly to plan, if her travel arrangements hadn't been suddenly altered. Bianca had intended to catch a scheduled flight back to England to spend a low-key Christmas at home. No fuss. No fanfare. She'd been looking forward to a bit of peace and quiet after the busy build-up to the royal wedding. Until her sister had forced her to accept an aeroplane ride from the last man she would ever have chosen to spend time with.

Just thinking about him made her shiver. Made her body tingle and her mouth grow dry.

Xanthos Antoniou.

The powerful Greek American billionaire who had proved to be an irresistible magnet to every woman under the age of ninety during the royal nuptials. Dazzlingly muscular, with sinful good looks, he had been like a dark meteor crash-landing into the golden splendour of the royal wedding. Nobody had been able to take their eyes off him. Herself included.

She hadn't known why her sister had been so insistent she accept a ride with him—especially when she'd made it quite clear she hadn't wanted to—but insistent she most certainly had been.

'Please, Bianca. As a favour to Corso. You'll get a lift in his private plane—*and* he's a crack pilot.'

Bianca had briefly wondered why her sister's royal husband was so keen to do Xanthos a favour, but at that point Rosie had rushed off to speak to someone else and it seemed the matter was closed. Which was why the man in question was currently heading purposefully in her direction across the marble foyer of the palace.

She tried not to glare as he made his way towards her, but keeping her expression neutral was a challenge. She didn't know what it was about the black-eyed billionaire which made her react so strongly, but she didn't seem able to control it. From the moment they'd first been introduced, she had felt a weird kind of reaction to him. A slow flush of heat to her cheeks. An uncomfortable awareness which made her breasts sting. Yet Xanthos Antoniou typified everything she disliked about the opposite sex. He exuded hard, masculine power and soft, sensual danger. He was alpha man personified. And those things did not turn her on.

She liked quiet men. Bookish men. Safe men.

Men who were the polar opposite of him. 'Bianca?'

His voice sounded like gravel being poured over honey as he said her name, which was presumably why her nipples had started pushing against her bra as if they wanted to escape from their lacy confinement and her heart to race as if she were running for a train. Breathing in, she curved her lips into the kind of polite smile she might have given a new client who had come seeking her legal advice.

'That's right. Bianca Forrester,' she replied briskly. Determined to put proceedings on a formal footing, she raised her eyebrows. 'I wasn't sure if you'd caught my surname when we were introduced yesterday, Mr Antoniou.'

'Oh, I never forget a surname, Ms Forrester,' he responded silkily. 'Just as it seems you haven't forgotten mine.'

But the mocking smile which accompanied his words made Bianca feel even more uncomfortable. She wasn't impressed by the fancy trappings of his wealth and couldn't care less that he had his own private jet. Her sister might have tried to big him up but she didn't want any part of it. She lowered her voice. 'Listen, I know you've been roped into offering me a lift and it's really very kind of you. But it won't be necessary.'

He frowned. 'Why not?'

'Because I already have a ticket and I'm perfectly happy to fly commercial. In fact, I'd prefer to travel that way. It means I can work on the flight, rather than have to make conversation.'

As her words clipped over him Xanthos felt a sudden flash of irritation because wasn't this scenario exactly what he had anticipated? It didn't matter that she was one of the most beautiful women he'd ever seen, with her coal-dark hair and eyes the colour of emeralds, the woman had attitude. The kind of attitude he didn't like. Cold and judgmental and...condescending. As if she'd already made up her mind about him and found him wanting.

And didn't that press all the wrong kinds of buttons? Didn't it remind him of where he had come from and why he was here?

'But your sister specifically asked me to ensure you got back to England safely,' he said coolly. 'And I could hardly ignore such a request, could I? Who could possibly refuse the new Queen?'

He didn't mention the other reason. The main reason. Which was his connection with the groom. The most powerful connection of all.

Blood.

The blood which bound the two men together, even though neither of them wished for that particular bond. It was the dark secret which smouldered in Xanthos's heart, reminding him of how deeply he had been betrayed. The secret which had taught him that no woman should ever be believed or trusted. For he was King Corso's half-brother and nobody else in the world knew, other than Bianca's sister, Rosie.

And that was the way both men wanted it to stay.

Xanthos didn't know why Corso had wanted him to attend his wedding and had initially refused the coveted invitation. But the King had pushed and pushed, and in the end Xanthos had let him have what he wanted. He suspected his half-brother wanted to keep him sweet and thus guarantee he would make no claim on the throne. But not only was Xanthos illegitimate, he had no desire for Corso's crown—or his kingdom. He couldn't think of anything worse than being a public figure. He liked his freedom and being answerable to nobody but himself. And if the last thing he wanted was to ferry the ungrateful Bianca Forrester home, he had given his word to her sister, and he was a man of his word.

But as he stared down into her dark-fringed eyes, an unwanted jolt of awareness reminded him of just how incredibly green they were and for a moment he was mesmerised by them, just as he was mesmerised by the soft pink lines of her lips and the undulating lines of her body. 'Are you ready?' he questioned unevenly.

'I don't think you understood what I just said.' The hands she held up in silent appeal did not minimise the patronising quality of her smile. 'I'm giving you a let-out.'

'But I don't want a let-out. The airport is swarming with paparazzi, which your sister thought you'd be keen to avoid.' This time he didn't bother to disguise his impatience. 'Most people would accept the offer of a lift in a private jet with good grace or even—dare I say it?—gratitude. So unless you want to make a scene, or to upset your sister on her honeymoon, I suggest you accompany me to the waiting car and we ride out to the airstrip.' His mouth hardened. 'Because the sooner we get going, the sooner this will be over.'

'You're making it sound as appealing as a trip to the dentist.'

He gave the ghost of a smile. 'Your words, Bianca, not mine.'

'Wow.' She flashed him a tight smile. 'This is going to be fun, isn't it?'

'I can barely contain my excitement.'

Past the giant fir tree they walked, with its spangle of silver stars and hundreds of tiny white lights which adorned the fragrant branches. Past boughs of holly and giant bunches of mistletoe. Past silver and golden balloons left over from the nuptials. The festive vibe of Christmas was still very much present, but Bianca was so riled by her companion's attitude that she barely took any notice.

Other guests stood chatting and they turned to watch as Bianca and Xanthos walked by.

'A striking couple,' Bianca overheard someone remark.

'Who *is* he?' someone else asked.

'I don't know, but she's a very lucky girl.'

But Bianca didn't feel in the least bit lucky as they sat in tense silence while the royal car whisked them to the airfield. She felt as if control had been snatched away from her and it was a sensation she didn't enjoy. The wind was a biting howl as she emerged from the limousine, and as a snowflake fluttered down and melted on her lips she saw Xanthos's dark gaze linger on her mouth, before he turned to speak to the driver. And the crazy thing was she *liked* him looking at her lips like that. She liked that sense of reluctance as he had dragged his gaze away and she couldn't understand why. How could you desire a man who made you feel so awkward and self-conscious? Hugging her coat around her, she followed him up the steps of the plane, ducking her head as she entered the cabin.

The interior of the aircraft was sleek and the fresh roses and glossy magazines gave the cabin a sumptuous feel, but it was smaller than she'd imagined and strangely silent. Had she been hoping for the distraction of other people? A co-pilot perhaps, or a gorgeous air stewardess or two, who might flirt with Xanthos and stop Bianca from entertaining her increasingly rogue thoughts about him.

'Aren't there any crew?'

'Nope. I'm flying solo. It's a relatively short flight and I think you'll find everything you could possibly need on board.' Dark eyebrows shot up to disappear into the ebony tangle of his hair. 'Unless you have a chronic need to be waited on? Is that what living in a palace does to you?'

'I don't actually live in the palace and I never did,' she returned. 'I used to spend my school holidays in a grace-and-favour house there because my father was an employee of the late King.'

'Then I'm sure you're perfectly capable of pouring your own champagne, Bianca,' he drawled, with a smile.

Was he aware of the impact of that smile? Did he realise that it made her want to shatter into pieces and then ask him to glue her back together? 'I only drink champagne when I'm celebrating,' she answered repressively. 'And the only thing I shall be celebrating is when we touch down.'

'Has anyone ever told you how ungrateful you are?'

'You have. I make that twice now. Has anyone ever told you how repetitive you can be, Xanthos?'

The ghost of a smile hovered around the edges of his sensual lips. 'No, I think you hold the record for making insulting observations,' he observed drily. 'So why don't you just read the safety card and buckle yourself in, while I prepare for take-off?'

Xanthos had been expecting yet more resistance, because she seemed determined to make this experience as difficult as possible. But to his amazement she was instantly compliant, removing her coat and reaching up to put it in the overhead locker—a movement which had the unfortunate side-effect of emphasising the luscious swell of her breasts. As she sank into her seat he lingered for a moment or two before heading for the flight deck, telling himself he needed to ensure she knew where the oxygen masks and life jackets were kept, but in reality it was more than safety concerns which kept him rooted to the spot. Because wasn't the bald truth that he was finding her intensely captivating?

Yesterday she had appeared as the bride's attendant, wearing a fitted red dress which had emphasised her ridiculously tiny waist and petite frame. Her black hair had been studded with scarlet roses and her lips had been scarlet, too, and she had looked like something out of an old-fashioned fairy tale. He'd noticed men sitting up bolt upright and watching her as she passed, her heavy silk gown brushing the stone cathedral floor, but she'd been too busy fiddling with her sister's heavy train to notice them. Or maybe she was one of those women who pretended to be ignorant of their own allure.

But today there was nothing remotely old-fashioned or fairy tale about her. The jeans and soft green sweater which clung to her curves were modern and practical. The thick waves of her black hair had been pulled back from her face and rippled in a ponytail down her back, and she appeared to be wearing little or no make-up. But with lashes that long and that black he guessed she didn't need to. Her only adornment was a pair of golden hooped earrings. No rings. No bracelets. She looked faintly forbidding and somehow unapproachable, and yet… He narrowed his eyes. Was it her lack of height—for she must be barely five feet four—which made her seem so provocatively feminine? Or was it her spirited attitude which he found so alluring?

Xanthos felt his heart miss an unexpected beat. Despite his professed disdain of women with attitude, it was a hypothetical rather than a real dislike, because it hardly ever happened. He was used to adoration and acquiescence. He'd never had to try very hard with women and sometimes he wondered what it would be like if he did.

But his momentary flicker of interest was quickly replaced with a sense of impatience. He didn't want to think this way about Bianca Forrester. In fact, he didn't want to think about her at all. She was the sister-in-law of his unacknowledged royal brother and, as such, she was nothing but a complication. All he needed to do was get through the next few hours before he was free of her and then on to Switzerland for some fun and games…

Sitting in the cockpit, he methodically went through his checklist before getting the all-clear from air traffic control and making a smooth ascent into the wide blue ribbon of the winter sky. He looked down as the famous red volcanic mountain of Monterosso grew ever smaller and thought it unlikely he would ever return, no matter how much Corso should try to persuade him otherwise. For he had no real desire to deepen the relationship with his brother. He did not want a newly discovered family, because families were nothing but a drain. They brought with them pain, and heartbreak, and disappointment. They had the power to wreck your whole life from the inside out. Who in their right mind would ever want a family?

He settled into what should have an uneventful flight and the journey proceeded with textbook ease—reminding him of the pleasure and satisfaction he always got from flying a plane.

And then, out of nowhere, things started to happen.

At thirty thousand feet, air traffic control informed him they could no longer get his flight read-out. He frowned. It should have just been a blip, but it wasn't. With mounting disbelief Xanthos watched as both transponders failed and then the radar flickered ominously before packing up completely. He felt the rush of adrenaline, but despite the tension in his body and mad race of his heart, he was strangely calm. Because, like every experienced pilot, he had trained for an eventuality such as this and was almost prepared for the sudden whiff of smoke from behind him and the thundering of feet as Bianca came running into the cockpit, her lips a gasping gash in her terrified face.

'S-smoke...' she managed and then again. 'Smoke!'

Quickly, Xanthos glanced over his shoulder and saw ominous grey clouds billowing from the bulkhead as the emergency systems suddenly kicked into overdrive. Alarm bells sounded and red lights were flashing and he went into crisis-management mode. Glancing down at his map, he calculated that the nearest airport was forty minutes away and knew an aircraft had twenty minutes' sustainability in case of fire. His mouth dried.

Twenty minutes.

He met the terror in Bianca's eyes as he punched out the four-digit Mayday signal and scanned the screen in front of him, his heart hammering with relief as he located a nearby disused airfield in the valley of a mountain.

'We need to make an emergency landing. Go back and strap yourself into your seat.

When I yell "brace" you do just that and we get off the plane asap. Leave everything behind. Do what I tell you and don't ask questions. Understand?'

To her credit she nodded and disappeared and then all Xanthos could think about was bringing down the craft safely, as he'd been taught. His concentration was total as they made a spiral descent and, just before bumping onto the icy runway, he yelled at Bianca to brace. The plane lurched and slid sideways on landing, careering towards the high white wall of a snowbank before coming to a juddering halt. And then he was charging into the cabin and undoing her seat belt and lifting her from her seat as smoke billowed all around them, making it hard to see.

He helped her outside into the bitter chill and never had it felt so wonderful to connect with the earth, even though the snow was hard and impacted like metal against his feet. For a moment it was difficult to keep his balance and he heard something like a sob escape from her lips. Their eyes met and something unfamiliar stirred deep inside him as he read the naked fear in hers. The need to protect her. To keep her safe. But first he had to get her away from the damned plane in case it exploded. Putting his arm tightly around her waist, he pulled her close, so close that her breath was warm against his cheek.

'Now run!' he yelled, leading her away across the runway, the cold wind leaving them both gasping for breath.

CHAPTER TWO

THE SENSATION OF Xanthos half carrying her across the airstrip was the only thing in Bianca's world which felt real right then. Everything else was like the worst disaster movie she'd ever seen. There was no colour in this unknown place, with its heavy grey sky and snowy landscape. No sound of traffic or birdsong—nothing but the wild howl of the wind as it whipped around them, with its icy fingers. The distant plane with its nose embedded in the snowbank added yet another nightmarish element and she wanted to scream and run as far away as possible— back to civilisation and everything she knew.

'L-let's get out of here!' she shouted, aware of his arm fixed firmly around her waist. 'Come on!'

But Xanthos didn't seem to be listening. He was scanning the area, as if committing every forbidding inch to memory. 'At least the smoke coming from the plane has subsided,' he said, almost reflectively. 'Which means it's unlikely to explode. We've been lucky.'

Lucky? Was he insane? Bianca stared at the distant aircraft. 'Please,' she whispered. 'I want to go.'

'Go where?'

'I don't know. Anywhere!' She looked around distractedly. 'There must be a village or town nearby. We need to go and find help!'

'No, we're not going to do that.'

His calmness was freaking her out and Bianca wondered if he'd bumped his head when he'd landed the plane during that scary descent, when the craft had been spinning like the slow cycle of a washing machine, leaving her dizzy with fear. Why was he refusing to see sense? Was she expected to take charge— as usual—and mightn't that be the best thing if Xanthos wasn't thinking straight?

'We must,' she said. 'We must!' In desperation she began to drum her bunched fists against the solid wall of his chest, but he didn't even seem to notice that either. 'I want to get away from here! As far away as possible.'

'You see that building over there?'

His continuing coolness had the effect of removing some of her panic and Bianca let her hands fall from his chest as she mirrored the direction of his glance to see a rudimentary stone building, topped with snow. It was possibly the most unwelcoming place she'd ever set eyes on and, instinctively, she shuddered.

'Of course I can see it.'

'That's where we're going.'

'If you think I'm setting foot in that place—'

'Now listen to me, Bianca,' he interrupted, his coolness now replaced by a grim note of determination. 'We can do this one of two ways. You can choose to walk with me and do what I tell you, which would be preferable. But if you continue to resist, I'll be forced to put you over my shoulder and carry you.'

'Because you want to prove how big and tough and macho you are?' she accused in a trembling voice.

'Because I've done enough survival training to know what I'm talking about and you've never been in a situation like this before.' He lowered his voice. 'Listen, I know you're in shock and I know the landing can't have been easy for you, but you need to take my advice.'

'Why should I? Twenty-four hours ago you were a total stranger to me—yet now I'm expected to depend on you for life and death decisions?'

'I'm afraid so.'

But maybe he registered the fear which was still trembling her voice because he reached out and pulled her towards him again and Bianca felt herself sinking into the hardness of his body. And she wanted this. Needed this. She wanted him to continue to hold her tightly because he felt warm and strong and dependable. As if he were her rock. Her anchor. And he was neither, she reminded herself severely, as she resisted the stupid desire to reach up and rest her cheek against his. He was someone she didn't particularly like and the feeling was obviously mutual.

'Let me go,' she said, without any real conviction.

He did exactly as she asked—and she was annoyed with herself for missing his touch—but when he next spoke, his voice had gentled by a fraction. 'You're going to have to trust me on this, Bianca. Do you think you can do that?'

Bianca chewed her lip, the irony of the situation not escaping her. One of the reasons she'd instinctively disliked Xanthos Antoniou was because she preferred men who were safe and she'd decided he wasn't. Yet right now she couldn't think of anyone safer, or anyone else she'd rather be with.

Wordlessly she nodded and began to follow him towards the small building which, on closer examination, appeared even more inhospitable than it had done from a distance. The stone walls were as grey as the darkening sky and she watched as he began shoving his shoulder against the wooden door in a brutal display of strength, until eventually it gave way with a damp-sounding creak and splintering noise. Cautiously, he entered the building with Bianca right behind him—not wanting to let him out of her sight. Her cheeks were burning with cold as she half stumbled into the welcome dryness and a huge cobweb floated onto her face. Instinctively, she brushed it away, her heart pounding with terror.

It took a moment for her eyes to become accustomed to the light. Not that there was much to see. The room obviously hadn't been used for a long, long time and had a damp, stale air about it. There was an empty desk with a wooden chair on either side and a battered armchair beside an old fireplace, which was lined with dust and ancient embers. The walls were bare, with pale rectangles where maps or photos might once have hung. In one corner, a narrow single bed was shoved up against the wall. In the other corner, a door led into a tiny room containing a toilet and a sink, above which hung a rusty mirror not much larger than a grapefruit. And that was it.

'What is this place?' she breathed.

'Obviously some kind of caretaker's hut which certainly won't be a match for the kind of luxury we experienced in Monterosso,' he observed drily. 'But we'll be protected from the elements, at least.'

Bianca began to shiver, realising that there'd been no time to grab her coat and that her sweater offered little protection against the clawing insistence of the icy temperature. 'Now what?' she whispered.

'You stay here. I'm going back to the plane—'

'No! Please.' The words sprang from her mouth before she could stop them. 'Don't leave me!'

His black eyes gleamed. 'A couple of hours ago you couldn't wait to see the back of me.'

'Don't remind me. Maybe if I'd listened to my instincts, I'd be safely back in London by now!'

'Good to see you're reverting to type, Bianca. We stand a much greater chance of survival if you're back to being your usual combative self—rather than some wilting little flower which needs tending all hours of the day and night.'

'I can assure you that wilting has never been part of my make-up.'

'I'm delighted to hear it. But you're cold. Look at you. You're shivering. You need warmth and so do I. Stay here,' he commanded softly as he pulled open the door. 'I'll be as fast as I can.'

She didn't know what made her say it. Was it the sudden tight clench of apprehension as she saw the forbidding bleakness of the winter landscape outside, or the fear of how she would cope if he didn't come back? Or was it the way he'd noticed that she was shivering and had ordered her to stay put, which seemed to introduce a level of intimacy which hadn't been there before?

'Be…careful.'

His mocking smile was unexpected and, again, she was reminded of its potency.

'How touching you should be so concerned for my welfare.'

'It's actually my own I'm worried about.'

The door slammed behind him and Bianca peered out through the window, watching him make his way across the airfield towards the crashed plane, his powerful body etched darkly against the bleached landscape as he negotiated the icy ground. It had started to snow again and already the light was beginning to fade. Soon it would be dark and at some point they would be expected to sleep. Her gaze swivelled to the narrow bed and ropey-looking mattress and she swallowed down the sudden lump of anxiety which had risen in her throat. How could two people possibly sleep on that?

She paced around the small room—mostly in an attempt to keep herself warm but also to try and make some sense of the thoughts which were spinning like cartwheels inside her head. As Xanthos had instructed, she'd left everything behind—but she dragged her phone from the back-pocket of her jeans, her heart sinking when she saw there was no signal. What a nightmare. She hadn't even asked any sensible questions about what their chances were, or whether anyone would ever find them.

And if they didn't?

She swallowed.

She wouldn't let herself go there.

She heard a pounding on the door—as if someone were kicking it—and she pulled it open to find Xanthos standing there, his hair covered in snow and his arms full of various paraphernalia. A blast of icy air followed him inside and she closed the door behind him as he unloaded most of the stuff onto the desk. He threw her overcoat across the room towards her, along with a dark scarf she recognised as his.

'Put those on,' he instructed tersely.

Although he was back in command mode, she was pleased enough to obey, doing up the buttons on the thick coat with unsteady fingers which felt like sticks of ice and then winding his soft scarf around her neck. Had the emergency fine-tuned her senses? Was that why she breathed in deeply, wanting to inhale the woody, masculine scent which seemed to have permeated the fine wool?

'Have you got gloves?' he demanded.

She nodded.

'Put those on too.'

She did as he asked while he slid on his own jacket and she couldn't seem to tear her eyes away from the powerful set of his shoulders and that broad chest.

'Stop staring and start unpacking,' he said abruptly, sliding his gaze towards her. 'I'm going back to the plane.'

'But why? You've only just got back!'

'Because, contrary to popular opinion, I'm not Superman. I couldn't carry everything in one trip. Just shut the door behind me, Bianca. I won't be long.'

This time she didn't beg him to stay, in fact she was pleased to see the back of him. *Stop staring*, indeed. But she had been, hadn't she? She'd been no better than all those women who'd been fawning over him at the wedding party last night. No wonder he was so arrogant.

She began to sort out the stuff he'd retrieved from the stricken aircraft, putting it into neat piles on the desk. Blankets, travel socks, a big container of water and, bizarrely, broken-off bits of rubber. When he reappeared, he was carrying her suitcase, and what looked like the entire contents of the minibar. 'I don't suppose you brought my hand luggage?' she questioned hopefully as he shut the door on the howling wind.

Xanthos felt a flicker of irritation flare up inside him. 'No, I did not bring your damned hand luggage,' he answered carefully. Was she expecting him to take a risk negotiating the treacherously icy airfield, just so she could get her manicured fingers on her no-doubt highly expensive face creams? Didn't she realise that from now on theirs was a new reality, where the pampered sister of the new Queen might be expected to rough it more than she was used to? Maybe he needed to spell it out for her.

They were going to be in close confinement for...how long? A pulse began to hammer at his temple. Who knew? But it was going to be difficult enough as it was. There was no point in falling out. He needed to forget her ingratitude and their mutual dislike, which had been simmering beneath the surface from the get-go. More importantly, he needed to ignore those wide-lashed eyes, which looked like green stars, and lose the memory of the red bridesmaid's dress which had outlined her tiny frame to perfection.

But wasn't it strange how sometimes your mind did exactly the opposite to what you wanted it to do? An image of creamy breasts constrained by blood-red satin swam into his head and, silently, he cursed. His libido might have chosen the most inconvenient of times to rear its head, but this was only going to work if he stopped thinking about her as a desirable woman. All he needed to focus on was the fact that she was the King's sister-in-law and that, somehow, he needed to keep her safe.

'I've just brought the essentials,' he elaborated. 'Why don't you start unpacking—while I go and investigate the bathroom?'

'Perhaps you'd like me to salute every time you shout out an order?' she demanded.

'Now that,' he said softly, 'would be something to see.'

Her sudden blush surprised him but he turned away from the arresting pinkness of her cheeks, shutting the bathroom door behind him with perhaps more force than was necessary. Inside the dingy washroom he located the stopcock, grateful he'd taught himself the practicalities of life, despite the immense wealth which had surrounded him until his ignominious fall from grace at the age of sixteen. But still it gave him pleasure knowing that he never paid anyone to do a job he wouldn't be able to do as well himself.

He checked everything was working and walked back into the hut, but although everything had been unpacked and was laid out with commendable neatness on the old desk, Bianca's face was set and tense, as if she'd been rehearsing what she was about to say.

'I need you to tell me what's happening,' she said, in a low voice.

'I've just made sure you have running water and a flushing toilet. Which must be some cause for celebration.'

'That's not what I meant.'

'No?' He raised his eyebrows.

Bianca felt the slow build of frustration. This was *exasperating*. And also confusing. She was a lawyer. She dealt with facts every day of her life. She asked incisive questions and had the ability to view a situation objectively. Yet now it felt as if her mind were composed of cotton wool and her normal powers of reasoning were slipping away from her. And you wouldn't need to be a genius to work out why.

It was him.

Without actually doing anything, he was unsettling her. Big time.

He was making her feel things which were disturbingly unfamiliar. Softly clawing, erotic things which were way out of her comfort zone. And she didn't want to feel this way. She didn't want to be aware of suddenly stinging breasts or the low curl of hunger deep inside her. Her focus should be on the gravity of their situation, not the curve of his sensual lips or the loud thundering of her heart.

She cleared her throat. 'My phone doesn't have a signal.'

'That's because there isn't one. I wouldn't expect there to be in a deserted mountainous region like this.'

'Are you trying to increase my anxiety levels, Xanthos?'

'No, I'm giving you the facts.' He fixed her with a speculative look. 'Or maybe you're someone who doesn't like dealing with facts?'

'I'm a lawyer.'

'Ah.'

'Go on,' she goaded. 'Say it.'

'Say what?'

'Make one of the many terrible jokes about lawyers which I've heard a zillion times before.'

'I wouldn't dream of it.' He slanted her the glimmer of a smile. 'Scoring points strikes me as something of a time-wasting exercise when we should probably be thinking about the night ahead.'

The night ahead. Cold and dark and miles from anywhere. Bianca drew in a deep breath as, once again, icy fear crept over her. 'How are you proposing we get out of here?' she croaked.

'We wait for someone to rescue us.' He glanced out of the window, where night had fallen, the thick snow clouds masking the stars with a dark mantle. 'Though I don't reckon it's going to be tonight.'

Bianca found herself wondering what lay out there in the impenetrable darkness and, despite the overcoat she was wearing, she gave a convulsive shiver. 'But how can we expect someone to rescue us if we haven't got a phone signal?'

'I sent out an emergency call just before I brought the plane down. They know we're here. We just have to be patient, Bianca. And survive.' His voice suddenly became harsh. 'That's really the only part which matters. That we make it through the night. Do you understand what I'm saying?'

His narrowed gaze was edged with doubt and Bianca knew she mustn't crumble. She mustn't let him see she was vulnerable, or scared—even if she was. She needed to be strong and independent—just as she'd been throughout her life.

'Yes, you're right,' she said, but suddenly it was very hard to stop her teeth from chattering. 'So what's the best way of ensuring we do? Survive, I mean?'

He reached over to grab a miniature bottle of whisky from the desk. 'Most of all, we need to keep warm.'

'I don't think drinking's a very good idea,' she said repressively. 'Isn't it counterproductive if we try to escape the reality of our situation by blotting it out with alcohol?'

He looked as if he were trying not to smile. 'I have no intention of hitting the spirits. I prefer my drinking companions to be a little less prickly around the edges. I was intending to use the Scotch as fuel—to help me start a fire. But first, I'll need to smash up those old chairs.'

She frowned. 'Isn't that criminal damage?'

'Technically, I suppose it is. Let them sue me.' His black eyes glinted as he headed for the door. 'Who knows? You might be called on to litigate in my favour, Bianca.'

Unsettled by his sarcasm, Bianca turned away as he went outside to demolish the chairs—smashing them against the stone walls of the hut, judging by the deafening noise he was making. But the jarring sound which had broken the silence of the night was the wake-up call she needed to shake her out of her shock. She couldn't allow Xanthos to do all the work, could she? For a start, it was much too cold to sit still, and maybe the gnawing fear which had taken root at the pit of her stomach would dissolve if she started being active and thought about something else.

She needed to consider how they were going to spend the long night ahead, and somehow that disturbed her almost as much as their isolation and the icy temperature of the room. The narrow bed seemed to be taunting her with all sorts of dangerous possibilities—and throwing into stark relief some of her own insecurities. She didn't *want* to think about the fact that this was the first time she'd ever contemplated spending the night with a man. She bit her lip. And that the circumstances couldn't be more bizarre.

So she set about keeping herself busy, shaking out the soft cashmere blankets Xanthos had brought from the plane and thinking what a contrast they made, laid out over the ancient mattress. Next she examined the selection of food he'd brought back from the plane—which was bizarre to say the least. She was just hunting around in her suitcase to locate her toothpaste and some clean underwear for the morning, when Xanthos returned bearing a commendable pile of firewood and suddenly she was stricken with embarrassment, her fingers closing over the little scrap of black silk, in a vain attempt to conceal her panties from him.

'Oh,' she said, her expression as self-conscious as her words. 'I wasn't expecting you back so soon.'

He kicked the door shut with more force than was necessary. 'You thought the night so pleasant I might want to linger?'

'No, of course not,' she said, stuffing the panties back inside the suitcase.

Xanthos put the wood down beside the fireplace, trying to forget what he'd just seen, telling himself he didn't give a damn what she wore next to her skin.

And you are a liar, taunted a mocking voice in his head. *Because of course you wanted to know and now you do.* Black and silky and lacy and surprisingly brief. Briefs for the lawyer. How appropriate.

The bland smile he offered her was supposed to reduce the sudden drying of his mouth, but unfortunately it did no such thing. Nor did it go any way towards alleviating the sudden aching at his groin. 'We need to build a fire,' he said roughly, perplexed by the effect she was having on him and wondering why he was so attracted to her. Because she wasn't like the other women who came into his orbit. She didn't bat her eyelashes, or simper, or smile. She didn't throw her head back and giggle uncontrollably whenever he said something mildly amusing. On the contrary. At times she seemed almost to be judging him—and not in a particularly positive way. Yet her green gaze was a temptation as well as a challenge and, no matter how hard he tried to fight it, he couldn't deny finding the tiny woman powerfully attractive, though he'd barely spoken to her before she'd been foisted on him today. He hadn't even asked her to dance at the reception last night and that had been a deliberate omission, despite her being the most beautiful woman in the room.

Was that because he'd known it made sense to keep his distance from someone unknowingly related to him by marriage? Or because some bone-deep instinct made him suspect that to touch her would be to make him lose his mind and, ultimately, control? And control was an essential component of his make-up. Once, it had been taken away from him and he had vowed it would never happen again. Which was why he always needed to be in charge. To be the decision maker. It was one of the elements of his character which had made him so successful in business. The same element which had left a litter of broken hearts behind him, because most women failed to understand the futility of attempting to control or to change him. They had an inability to accept him as the man he was. Instead they tried to tie him down and stultify him with a domesticity he had no appetite for.

Crumpling up one of the magazines, he laid it in the grate, wondering how he was going to endure the hours which lay ahead, unable to blot out the images which were streaming into his mind with disturbing clarity. Of *course* getting up close and personal with Bianca would make the time pass more quickly, but that wasn't going to happen. He was stuck here with her for the foreseeable and didn't intend saying or doing anything he might later regret.

For tonight, at least, there was no escape from the green-eyed temptress and he was just going to have to get by the best way he could.

He struck the first match.

Because no way was he going to have sex with her.

CHAPTER THREE

HE LIT A fire and it was the sexiest thing Bianca had ever witnessed.

Her throat tightened and so did her breasts. She knew Scouts were supposed to be able to create fire by rubbing two sticks together and she'd always thought it a bit of a myth.

But Xanthos was doing something on exactly those lines. Not with sticks, but with some alcohol-soaked wood from the chair he'd smashed up, along with bits of rubber he'd retrieved from the plane. One minute the temperature had been sub-zero and the next, he'd conjured up roaring flames which were licking at her skin with seductively warm tongues. As the flames engulfed the whisky-soaked pieces of wood the dank interior of their shelter suddenly felt almost luxurious. Warm colours of coral and gold were splashed over the walls and the fire's crackle was almost hypnotic.

'Wow,' she said, her voice full of unwilling admiration as he stood up from his crouching position.

'You like that?' he questioned softly, stepping back to survey the result of his endeavours, and Bianca wished he hadn't because now he was standing beside her and her body had begun to react to the proximity of his. The fire had magnified his shadow and thrown it into stark relief, so that it dominated the room with its darkness. He was so tall and so muscular, radiating a powerful energy she'd never come across before, and she could feel the slow curl of something sweet and insistent deep inside her, something she realised was desire.

She nodded. 'It's amazing,' she said, through lips which had grown annoyingly dry.

She still couldn't really relax around him, but she couldn't deny that his behaviour was a dramatic departure from her expectations of him. She'd had him down as yet another arrogant man with more money than was good for him, who just waved an entitled hand to get people to do his bidding. She'd pictured his life as smooth and effortless—screened from the nitty-gritty of the real world in some chic New York penthouse. Yet here he was in this derelict old building, creating fire out of practically nothing but the dextrous flick of his fingers.

Fire-making was a primitive skill, she acknowledged reluctantly. It spoke to her on an elemental level she couldn't seem to understand. Everything seemed to have slowed down, and her senses had become raw. She could hear the crackle of the fire and smell the woodiness of the smoke. She thought how ironic it was that fire could be their saviour as well as their enemy. For the first time since the plane had crashed, she felt warm—and safe. That was the craziest thing of all. With him she felt safe.

But the plane *had* crashed, she reminded herself. Surely they shouldn't just be lazing around like this as if they were on some unexpected glamping vacation? So do something. Take back some of the control you seem to have relinquished so willingly to Xanthos Antoniou.

Because independence was the only thing she'd ever been able to rely on, after her father's terrible accident. Her mother and sister had been in bits and started to lean on her, until it had become a habit for them all. Yet she recognised that there was a certain comfort to be derived from being the one who always made the decisions. It was Bianca who had concluded at a family conference that it was best to switch off her father's life support after years of being hooked to a ventilator, with her mother tearfully agreeing. After that Bianca had concluded she could survive anything life threw at her, if she had all the facts at her fingertips and kept her emotions in check.

She cleared her throat. 'Shouldn't we be trying to attract attention?'

He shot her a questioning look. 'And how do you suggest we do that?'

'I don't know. Have you…um…' she shrugged her shoulders a little helplessly '…thought about lighting a fire outside?'

'No, I haven't. Because only an idiot would do that. It's dark, it's deserted and we're in the valley of a mountain, in case you hadn't noticed. Even in the unlikely event that someone might see us, I'd probably freeze to death making the effort.' His dark eyes glittered with an emotion she couldn't make out. 'And while I appreciate I'm not your ideal choice of companion, presumably even you aren't hard-hearted enough to wish me dead?'

His remark hit home. Of course it did. Quickly, Bianca glanced out of the window, determined he shouldn't see her expression and realise that he had the power to hurt her. Did he think she was hard-hearted? A flicker of insecurity ran through her. Was that the person she had become? A cold and controlling robot? She clenched her fingers, trying to quash her suddenly rampant feelings of self-doubt. No, it was not. She was just careful, that was all. She protected herself against the heartache which other women just seemed to lay themselves open to, because she'd learnt that nothing was as bad as emotional pain. But maybe she had taken self-protection just a step too far and now was the time to be conciliatory. 'Don't be ridiculous.' She drew in a deep breath. 'If you must know, I'm very...grateful for everything you've done.'

Their eyes met. Held. Was she imagining the flicker of something responsive in his? Some glint of fire in their ebony depths which made her heart clench with pleasure. For one crazy moment she thought he was about to reach out and touch her, but all he was doing was looking at her and she found his dark gaze immeasurably comforting. It felt like an innocent form of intimacy, if there was such a thing. Was that why she blurted out the first thing which came into her head?

'Why don't I make us some tea? When I was unpacking the provisions, I noticed you'd brought an ice bucket from the plane, presumably to hold water. We could boil some up on the fire and use some of those peppermint teabags.'

'Resourceful,' he murmured.

'You sound surprised.'

'Maybe I am. Maybe I'm used to women who like to be waited on.' He slanted her a smile as she carefully positioned the bucket on top of the smouldering logs. 'Why don't I watch that for you?' he suggested. 'You might want to go and wash that smear off your face.'

Smear? Instinctively, she reached her fingertips to her face. What smear? Grabbing her soap bag, Bianca hurried into the bathroom and shut the door, her heart beating very fast as she stared into the tiny mirror and saw the large dark mark on her cheek, which must have resulted from her earlier close encounter with a cobweb. Not a pretty sight. Maybe that was why he had been staring at her so intently. Of course it was. In which case, she really needed to lose the schoolgirl fantasies about him, as of now. She washed her face— but the water was icy cold, the soap failed to lather and, of course, she had no towel. She patted her cheeks dry with her hands and then brushed her teeth, ignoring the taunting voice which demanded to know why she thought that necessary.

Then she freed her hair from its ponytail and began to brush it out, convincing herself it would be warmer to leave it loose. But there were other justifications for allowing the ebony waves to fall over her shoulders in a glossy tumble. She stared back at her grapefruit-sized reflection with a touch of defiant feminine pride. Wasn't the truth that she wanted to look good, because that would make her *feel* good about herself and give her back some of the confidence which seemed to be in short supply? She felt awkward in the company of Xanthos—as if she didn't quite know how to behave around him. Somehow, the powers of reasoning— which had always been her calling card— had slipped away from her. And she needed to get them back.

With a resolute air, she reknotted the

scarf he'd given her and returned to find him sprawled on the floor beside the fire, as the water bubbled up to a boil. Did he have any idea how gorgeous he looked? His long legs were spread out in front of him—the faded denim pulled taut over the definition of powerfully-muscular thighs. Her heart gave a mighty kick and it took a huge effort to drag her gaze away, especially when he leaned over to remove the bucket of boiling water from the fire.

Focus, she told herself severely. Just focus.

Working as efficiently as she could with limited resources, she dunked peppermint teabags in two incongruously delicate bone-china mugs which must also have come from the luxury aircraft. She handed one to Xanthos, which he took with a nod of thanks, before perching with her own on the edge of the armchair, which he had pulled closer to the fire. She cradled the cup between her hands and took a sip, thinking how the simple pleasure of being warm again could make her temporarily forget the precariousness of their situation. 'Mmm…good, isn't it?'

But he didn't respond as he sipped his own tea—he seemed lost in thought. And as Bianca put her cup down and sneaked a glance at her watch, a sudden sense of isolation hit her, along with a hefty dose of realisation. It was only just gone eight o'clock and although she was amazed how much time had passed, and even if they were rescued at first light—*if*—there were still hours to get through. With him.

He was staring into the fire, the firelight licking at his hard profile and highlighting his body in red and shadowed detail. She thought that he managed to look both relaxed yet alert to danger—like a jungle cat which had momentarily ceased its relentless prowling. He represented all the things she inherently shied away from and yet Bianca was aware that her feelings towards him were changing. Was that because he had taken command of them both in a life-threatening situation and somehow made her feel secure?

She wasn't used to a man making decisions on her behalf yet, disturbingly, she was finding she rather liked it. His imperturbable manner was almost as attractive as his undeniable good looks, and she was rapidly becoming aware that Xanthos Antoniou was the kind of man who could burrow underneath her defences. Was that what was happening to her? Was that why all she could think about was wanting to *touch* him—to run her fingertips over that hard body in a slow and very thorough exploration? She wanted to break the rule of a lifetime. To find out if he could possibly feel as good as he looked. To discover whether his skin really *was* like silk, or the honed ridges of muscle as rock-like as they seemed.

And she had to call a halt to what was nothing but madness. She had to change the dynamic between them, as of now. To move from infatuation to impartiality.

But how? Her flippancy and stonewalling of earlier hadn't worked, had they? If anything it had only increased the spiralling tension between them. It had created a dialogue which bordered on flirtation. So try something different. Pretend he's a colleague you've met at some out-of-town conference. Pretend he's got a wife and two children waiting for him at home. Do that chatty, superficial thing—knowing that once this is over, you need never see one another again. Leaning back in the battered armchair, she tucked up her legs beneath her, and slanted him a companionable smile. 'Well, I must say, this is the last place I ever imagined spending Christmas.'

He lifted his arms above his head to give a

slow stretch and Bianca found herself thinking that none of her work colleagues had ever
displayed a physique as achingly muscular
as his.

'Ditto,' he growled.

She cleared her throat. 'What are you supposed to be doing for the holidays?'

Dark eyebrows were elevated. 'Do you really want to know?'

Bianca felt an unexpected flutter of
nerves. 'Of course,' she affirmed brightly.
'And after all, what else are we going to talk
about? The likelihood of anyone ever finding us? The rapidly plummeting temperature outside?'

Or the most pressing question of all, Xanthos thought grimly. Which was, where the
hell were they going to sleep? And how was
that going to happen when his groin felt so
heavy that he could barely move? He sighed.
Better to humour her, he supposed—while
remaining as detached as possible. Which
meant ignoring the shapely legs she'd just
crossed, sending a battery of erotic thoughts
fizzing to his starved senses. Maybe the
boredom of making small talk would help
him forget how much he wanted to kiss
her. 'I was intending to catch up with some

friends in Geneva for a short skiing break. I'm supposed to be meeting them on Christmas Eve.'

'That's tomorrow.'

'I know when it is, Bianca.'

'Do you think they'll miss you?'

He thought about Kiki—the supermodel he'd met briefly in Monaco last summer, who had been chasing down a meeting with him ever since. She would certainly miss him. But disconcertingly, he wasn't the least bit disappointed at passing up on what could have been a delicious booty call, not even when he thought about the model's traffic-stopping long legs and her stunning blonde beauty, which had graced the covers of so many magazines. Was that because, in the here and now, the voluptuous frame of the petite Bianca curled up in the armchair opposite was a far more tantalising prospect?

'I'm pretty sure they will,' he said wryly. 'But since I'm hoping we might be rescued before that happens, I might still make the slopes for Christmas morning.' He forced himself to enquire about her own plans, reminding himself that women liked to talk about themselves, which would curtail the inevitable questions she might ask him. Because he didn't like answering questions. He preferred enigma to openness. More importantly, he didn't want her to know who he really was. He had no desire to open that particular can of worms.

His mouth twisted. The truth of his conception had sickened him—coating his already difficult past with yet another unsavoury layer. He had thought it might be possible to overcome it, wondering if Corso's persuasive words were true and that maybe they could form some kind of relationship. But deep in his heart he knew that was never going to happen. He should never have gone to the wedding. Should never have agreed to see his brother again. He had felt like a fish out of water. He didn't need Corso. He didn't need anyone.

'What about your own plans?' he asked.

'Oh, very quiet. Just me. Well, I had a couple of invitations from friends to spend the day with them, but you know what it's like…' She shrugged. 'I'm not really a big fan of the holiday.'

'You don't like Christmas?'

'Well, that's going a bit far. It's just never really meant very much to me. Not like it does to other people. It's mostly about family, isn't it?'

'But you have your sister. And your mother was at the wedding, wasn't she?'

'Yes, with my aunt. They're both staying on at the palace to be waited on hand and foot, while Rosie and Corso are on honeymoon. They wanted me to join them, but I said no.'

He raised his eyebrows. 'Because the idea didn't appeal to you?'

Bianca stared briefly into the golden-red heart of the fire, wondering if he was actually interested in her answer or whether, like her, he was simply going through the motions of conversation. The latter, she suspected. But surely it was safer to concentrate on the subject of Christmas, rather than on her hardening nipples, which were thankfully hidden by her overcoat. 'Not really,' she admitted. 'I used to spend the holidays in Monterosso when I was growing up and—well, so much has changed. I never particularly enjoyed my Christmases there. They always seemed to be about the royal family and nobody else. And I didn't want…' She hesitated. 'I had no desire to go back there.'

'No. I can understand that. Connecting with the past is often difficult.'

It was an observation she wasn't expecting him to make and although she wanted to know more about what had made him say it, something told Bianca to hold the growing silence, to let *him* be the one to break it.

'What was it like as a child in Monterosso?' he questioned at last. 'Did you spend Christmas with Corso and his family?'

'Gosh, no, nothing like that,' she said slowly. 'Our worlds were miles apart. Inevitably. He was the Crown Prince, and although my father might have been the palace archivist, essentially, he was still a servant. And the late King was a stickler for protocol.'

'Was he?' he questioned, and Bianca realised that his voice had grown very harsh. 'Was he really?'

'Oh, yes. He was very particular about everyone knowing their place. All the cooks and butlers and maids used to be working round the clock for days leading up to the holiday.' She hesitated as her mind took her back. 'But he used to throw a party for all the palace staff at lunchtime on Christmas Eve. It was all very old-fashioned. And afterwards we would all gather round the tree and be given our presents from the King.' She remembered how much she'd hated that sense of being an inferior. The sense of being a recipient of the King's patronage and having to be excessively *grateful* for everything which came her way. Hadn't it been that which had spurred her on to work so hard at school and forge for herself her own career, knowing that financial and emotional independence were more important to her than anything?

'And did you like him?' he questioned suddenly. 'The King?'

'Did I like him?' she repeated slowly. 'I've never really thought about it before. He was just there. Ruling everything and everyone. His power was absolute.' But as Xanthos continued to regard her curiously, she knew she was short-changing him. And since she would never see him again once they were rescued—*if* they were rescued—why not articulate something she could easily tell a stranger, but would never admit to her sister or her mother? 'I didn't really like him, no. He was a cold, cruel man and sometimes I felt sorry for Corso.'

'Why would you feel sorry for the sole heir to such a wealthy kingdom?' he demanded. 'A man who would one day have untold wealth and power at his fingertips.'

She wondered what had caused that sudden bitterness to enter his voice. 'His mother died when he was young and I think... I think that hit him very hard,' she explained falteringly. 'He used to come to our house and have meals with us sometimes, and I used to get the feeling that those times with our family were the only warmth and real company he'd ever known.'

'Lucky Corso,' he said hollowly.

'Maybe.' She hesitated. 'You haven't said how you know the King.'

'No.' There was a pause. 'Let's just say we have business interests in common.'

But he didn't do the polite thing of elaborating on what those interests might be, even though Bianca sat there in silence, giving him the perfect opportunity to tell her. Instead, he scrambled to his feet and once again, his shadow seemed to devour the entire room with its darkness.

'At some point we should eat,' he said, his voice assuming a familiar note of command. 'It'll pass the time as well as keeping our strength up. I'll fix us something.'

He was doing it *again*. Taking charge and

assuming control. And even though it might be a very old-fashioned way to behave, Bianca was finding it dangerously seductive. So don't let him get to you. Show him that you're perfectly capable of looking after yourself.

She stood up, feeling immediately dwarfed by his immense height. 'That's okay. I can just as easily do it.' She gave him a polite smile. 'Why don't you let me fix something while you tend the fire?'

'Why don't I?' he echoed as he bent down to pick up a log.

Glad for the distraction, Bianca went over to the desk and rifled through one of the boxes. 'Caviar, chocolate, fine wine,' she listed. 'Perfect for upmarket snacking on luxury jets, but not exactly what you'd call a balanced diet. Still, I suppose it'll have to do.'

She did her best, smearing the costly black caviar onto crackers and arranging them on bone-china plates in as attractive a way as possible. She spread the bizarre feast out in front of the fire and sat down while Xanthos walked over to the desk and pulled out a half-bottle of champagne, his black eyes mocking in the firelight as he held it up. 'Something to help wash it down, or are you still vetoing alcohol?'

Bianca shrugged, not objecting when he tipped the fizzy wine into her empty teacup and handed it to her. 'Peppermint-flavoured champagne,' she commented wryly, as she took a sip.

'Could be the next big thing,' he murmured, before flicking her a shuttered glance. 'By the way, thanks for dinner. Under the circumstances, it looks delicious.'

His unexpected praise pleased her and for a while they ate and drank in a silence which was almost companionable. As the fire warmed her skin and the luxury food provided a burst of energy, Bianca could almost have forgotten about their predicament. But she couldn't ignore the subject they hadn't yet discussed. The invisible elephant in the room, which was now looming so huge that it seemed to be sucking all the available oxygen from the air.

'So.' She surveyed the hard set of his profile and tried not to wonder what it would be like to kiss him. 'Where are we going to sleep?'

He turned to face her, his expression unreadable. 'I would have thought the answer was obvious. There's a bed over there.'

'I can see that for myself.' She sucked in a deep breath. 'And since it's a bed for one person, that creates a bit of a problem.'

'Does it?'

'Of course it does.'

Xanthos could see which way this was going and kept his tone studiedly casual. 'So you'd like me to sleep on the stone floor, would you, Bianca?'

She shrugged awkwardly. 'Obviously it isn't ideal.'

'Damned right it isn't ideal,' he snapped, thinking what a spoiled little princess she could be— despite her protestations that she was nothing but a royal servant's daughter. 'Sooner rather than later that fire is going to die out and we need to conserve our fuel because we don't know when we're going to be rescued.' He thought how confident he sounded about the possibility of someone getting to them in time.

Because what if nobody did?

But surely it was easier to concentrate on practicalities rather than his incipient desire for this woman, which was building by the second. A desire to crush those pink lips beneath his and to kiss her until they were both gasping for breath. To explore her luscious curves, which were currently sending out a siren call to his starving senses. He clenched his fists so hard that the knuckles cracked, because this was madness.

He wanted Bianca Forrester, yes. At this precise moment he couldn't remember ever wanting a woman quite as much. He wanted her with a hunger which felt raw and visceral, and he wondered if their life-threatening incarceration was intensifying a desire which was obviously mutual. His mouth hardened. He had seen the way her gaze had roved hungrily over him earlier, her emerald eyes darkening in the firelight. But he forced himself to think rationally—because wanting a woman and having sex with her were two very different things. And denial was no hardship for a man who liked to test himself.

He raised his arms above his head to fabricate a yawn. 'Every survival manual printed will tell you that the best way to keep warm is for our bodies to be in close contact. It's also the best way to maximise the blankets we have,' he drawled. 'Which is why we're going to share that bed.'

'Are you completely crazy?'

'What's the matter, Bianca? You reckon you're so irresistible I won't be able to keep my hands off you?'

'That's not what I said.'

'No, but it's what you implied.'

Their eyes clashed and Xanthos knew he had to come clean, because what other choice did he have? He couldn't just walk away from her. Couldn't plead business, or a meeting, or the need for an early night—or any of the other strategies he used whenever a woman was starting to burrow beneath his defences. 'Look, I can't deny finding you attractive,' he admitted slowly. 'Why wouldn't I? You're a very beautiful woman and you've got a lot going for you. But you're not my type—and I don't have sex with women just for the sake of it. I grew out of that a long time ago.'

She was shaking her head with what looked like fury, so that her hair rippled like glossy jet in the firelight. 'You think I'd ever have sex with *you*?' she flared back. 'Why, I'd rather walk barefoot through the snowy mountains of this godforsaken country to try to find my way back to Monterosso before I did that!'

'Perfect. Then we're both of the same accord. You don't want to have sex with me and

I don't want to have sex with you. What could be simpler?' He splayed out his palms and held them in front of the flicker of flames. 'Which means we can share that bed over there with impunity.'

CHAPTER FOUR

His body was warm and hard and strong. His arms were clasped tightly around her waist.

It felt like heaven.

It felt like hell.

Bianca sucked in a disbelieving breath as her eyes fluttered open and she took in the full extent of her predicament—if such a situation could ever be described as a predicament.

She was in bed with Xanthos Antoniou. Lying wrapped in his arms, actually, beneath a pile of blankets whose cashmere luxury was at odds with their derelict surroundings. She could feel hard, honed muscle pressing against her. The circle of his arms enclosing her. Keeping her safe. Because—against all the odds—hadn't she just enjoyed the most incredible sleep of her life, despite the fact of being stuck out in the middle of nowhere?

The middle of nowhere. She stiffened. *With a man who was dangerously sexy.*

'Relax,' came a rich voice from beside her. 'It wasn't that bad, was it?'

She turned to see his face mere inches away from hers, strong jaw shadowed with new growth, black eyes narrowed and watchful. Desperately, she tried not to let her panic show, but the panic was there, all right, and it was rising by the second. And who could blame her? She'd slept with a man for the first time in her life and couldn't remember a single thing about it.

Surreptitiously touching her palms to her thighs, she was relieved to discover she was still wearing her jeans. She wriggled her toes. Bed socks, too. And her thick jumper. And even... Her fingertips moved exploratively over her torso as they began to explore an unfamiliar fabric. It felt like a fleece, which must belong to him because she had never owned such a thing.

'What wasn't that bad?' she demanded, her imagination still playing tricks on her.

'Sharing a bed with me.' His black eyes glittered. 'Don't worry, Bianca, your honour remains intact.'

'That's not what I meant!'

'Sure it was.' He gave a lazy smile. 'So why not look on the bright side? We kept warm and we stayed alive, and that was our main objective.'

She supposed he was right. Fractured memories of the night returned to haunt her, like a shattered mirror being pieced back together. She remembered a bizarre supper of caviar and chocolate. A cup of champagne, which had tasted like toothpaste. The awkwardness of who was going to use the bathroom first. Well, awkward for her, since she'd never shared a bathroom with a man before but she hadn't liked to say so. And then there had been the bed. She remembered him stating how they must conserve fuel and it would lower their chances of survival if they halved the meagre supply of blankets and then froze to death as a result. He had made sharing body heat seem like a necessity rather than a pleasure.

But it *had* been a pleasure, hadn't it? That was the awful truth of it. It still was, even though they were bundled up in warm clothes and their faces and their hands were the only pieces of flesh on show. She knew she ought to get out of bed, but she felt so deliciously warm and secure that she was reluctant to move anywhere. Her position could almost have been described as comfortable, were it not for the distracting thud of a pulse at her groin and the small matter of her breasts. Well, not so small actually. They seemed to have swollen to twice their normal size and were extremely tender as she lay glued against him.

She wondered what he would say if she asked him to kiss her, then silently cursed herself for thinking such a thing. Because hadn't he stated most emphatically last night that she wasn't his type, which was presumably why he hadn't touched her in any way which could be considered inappropriate. She chewed on her lip. He had somehow managed to turn what could have been a very awkward encounter into something which had left her wistful and aching for something she seemed to have been denied.

'I suppose we ought to get up,' she said half-heartedly, hoping he might try to change her mind.

Xanthos nodded, forcing himself to pull away, resisting the temptation to explore the compact little body which had been pressing so provocatively against him all night long, sending out the unmistakable message that she was as aroused as he was. Her green eyes were wide, the pupils dark and dilated, and her bottom lip was trembling, no matter how hard she dug those little white teeth into the rosy cushion to try to curtail it. He thought how easy it would be to kiss her. And then? His mouth hardened, rivalling the persistent ache at his groin. Did he really want to complicate an already complicated situation by having sex with her, despite all his protestations that she wasn't his type?

He nodded. 'Good idea. Why don't you go and…?' Was that really his voice? So slow and so heavy, as if he were speaking underwater. 'Use the bathroom first?'

'Okay.'

He missed her softness the moment she slid from the narrow bed, forcing himself to close his eyes as she made her way towards the bathroom—because visual stimulus was the last thing he needed to add to his already overloaded senses.

When the door had slammed shut behind her, Xanthos remained exactly where he was, willing the exquisite aching of his erection to subside, though for once his body was refusing to obey him. He wondered if Bianca had any idea of the torture she'd put him through during what had felt like the longest night of his life. She had slept deeply. He had not. After an initial tense silence when he had joined her on the narrow mattress, she had fallen asleep surprisingly quickly, her head falling innocently against his shoulder. And that was when his torture had begun.

He had endured her cosying up to him as if he were a giant hot-water bottle and pressing herself against him. Endured? Who was he kidding? It had been the ultimate sensation of frustration and fantasy—and a surprisingly potent mix. The gravity of their situation had temporarily dissolved as he had inhaled the shampoo sweetness of her hair and felt her dewy cheek resting against his. He wondered if his newly awoken desire had anything to do with the fact that she had confounded all his expectations of her, proving herself to be both resourceful and not afraid of taking on her share of the work.

And he had enjoyed holding her. A surprising discovery for someone who had never shared a bed with a woman without having sex with her. Yet the chasteness of their situation had inspired a fierce sense of protectiveness in him. Some primitive instinct had kept him alert and watchful, knowing he needed

to keep her safe. He had lain awake for countless minutes, listening to the steady beat of
his heart and thinking that here, in this bare,
bleak room, life had suddenly acquired a fundamental simplicity. If you discounted the
immediate and present danger, it provided
a strange kind of comfort to realise that the
stresses of the modern world had receded—
and one in particular.

The unsettling discovery about his birth
had been digging insistently at the back of his
mind ever since Corso had turned up in New
York last year, and he'd been confronted with
the reality that he had a brother, of sorts. Not
just any brother, but one who was now a king.
It had troubled him on many levels, not least
because essentially Xanthos was a loner. A
very private man with no desire to endure any
of the problems brought about by families.

But in this bleak mountain hideaway he
had discovered a curious kind of peace. It was
almost as if he had been given a clean slate
to start over. With his arm around Bianca's
waist, he had watched the snow clouds clear
to reveal an indigo sky, pricked with the diamond glitter of stars. As a cold, pale dawn
had illuminated the stone floor and the sheen
of her ebony hair, he had wondered what the

day had in store for them. And instead of dread he had felt nothing but expectation, and acceptance.

He could hear the sound of running water next door as he got out of bed and busied himself with making a new fire, so that by the time Bianca walked back in, the temperature of the room had lost some of its icy edge. Her face was shiny-clean, her hair a glossy bounce. She'd put on a sweater the colour of a sunrise, blue jeans were hugging her hips and Xanthos couldn't help acknowledging just how...*amazing* she looked. Fresh, yet hot. It was yet another unwanted punch to his jangled senses and, cursing the sudden erotic trajectory of his thoughts, he rose to his feet.

'I'll use the bathroom,' he said abruptly. 'Just keep the fire going.'

'Of course.'

At least the icy temperature of the water was enough to restore his equilibrium and he washed and dressed as quickly as possible. By the time he returned, Bianca was staring out of the window and she turned round as he entered.

'I want to talk to you.'

'So talk.'

Her green eyes were very clear and un-blinking. 'Do you think—?'

He could hear the sudden fear which had entered her voice and she hesitated, looking around at the bare, bleak walls as if she were seeing them for the first time. Her mask of bravado had slipped to reveal the frightened woman beneath and Xanthos felt his heart go out to her. He walked across the room to-wards her, resisting the desire to pull her into his arms—framing her cheek with the palm of his hand instead.

'If you're about to ask me whether I think anyone's going to find us, the answer is that I don't know,' he said softly. 'But I do know it's pointless worrying about things we can't control.'

'What, so we just sit here and *wait*?'

'Not necessarily. We could go outside and walk.'

'Yeah.' Her gaze was darting around the tiny dimensions of the room as if it were a prison. 'I feel as if I'll go crazy if we have to spend much longer in here.'

'Come on, then.'

They pulled on extra clothing and she reached for a bobble hat and gloves, before they stepped out into the freezing morning and a very different world from the one which had greeted them the day before.

For a moment Xanthos just drank it in. Gone were the oppressive grey clouds and icy flakes which had swirled so relentlessly from the sky. In the sunlight, the snow was glistening, turning the high bank into a glitter of whiteness. Behind them the peak of the huge mountain soared up into a cloudless blue sky. Even the crashed plane seemed to have lost its ability to shock or terrify. Total silence engulfed them.

'It's…beautiful,' breathed Bianca, at last.

Yes. Very. Just like her. Xanthos felt the sudden beat of his heart as he met her emerald gaze beneath the brim of her grey bobble hat. The most beautiful woman he'd ever laid eyes on and, ironically, the last woman he might ever see. He thought about the restraint he'd employed throughout that long night and the effort it had cost him. There had been yet more restraint this morning, when she had brushed her lips over his jaw, and if she hadn't been asleep he might have kissed her back. It had been a masterclass in self-discipline from which he had derived a certain amount of masochistic pleasure, but now he wondered whether he should have instigated something else.

If he were to die here in this valley—would that be his one regret? That he *hadn't* had sex with Bianca Forrester?

'Come on. Let's walk,' he said abruptly. 'We need to keep moving.'

He was careful not to let them stray too far from the hut and when he noticed her start to shiver, insisted they go back inside, where he stoked up the fire and made more tea while she doled out squares of dark chocolate, which they ate mechanically. Yet as the minutes ticked by, he could feel the tension mounting in that small room and it wasn't just the unspoken fear that they might never be rescued. Desire shimmered in the air—so real it was almost tangible.

'Maybe we should try and read to pass the time,' she said, her prim words shattering his erotic thoughts. 'Do you have any novels with you, Xanthos?'

'You go ahead and read,' he growled. 'I'm going to take that desk outside and dismantle it for firewood.'

She raised her eyebrows. 'Is that really necessary?'

'You think I just like breaking up furniture

for the hell of it?' He stared her down. 'That I'm channelling my inner caveman?'

'I have no idea.' She met his gaze with a look of challenge. 'Are you?'

But despite his words, the action of smashing the desk to pieces was infinitely satisfying and not just because it was so alien to the way he lived in New York. The physical exertion sublimated some of his sexual hunger and his brief exhilaration was compounded when he heard a sound in the distance. At first he wondered if he had imagined it. It seemed too faint to be real, yet in the overwhelming silence of that stark white world it was as deafening as a bolt of thunder. He stood stock-still as it increased in volume and that was when he yelled at the top of his voice. 'Bianca!'

Dark hair flying, she came running out—her gaze swiftly taking in the approaching vehicle before looking into his face, as if seeking confirmation. And when he nodded, they both looked upwards—towards the steep road which wound down the side of the mountain, where a sturdy-looking vehicle was making slow but steady progress towards them.

'Xanthos,' she said, her thin whisper hopeful on the frozen air.

'Yes,' he said simply.

She reached out to clutch his arm for support—as if without it she might slip to the snowy ground. Was that why he clamped his fingers over hers, to anchor her—or was it simply because he wanted the opportunity to touch her again? Her hand felt tiny beneath his palm and the touch of her gloved fingers pressing against his jacket made it seem like a double dose of sensuality.

They watched in silence as the vehicle slowly made its way towards them, not wanting to jinx it. As if words might reveal the Jeep to be nothing but an apparition—a wintry mirage which would merge into the bleached landscape and disappear. But the sounds grew louder. The hefty chains on the thick tyres were making easy work of the frozen road. Eventually it bumped its way down onto the airfield and the craziest thing was that all Xanthos wanted was to pull Bianca into his arms and kiss the breath out of her. To ask if they could have a few minutes alone, so that he could take her back inside that hut and do what he should have done last night.

But he gently disengaged her fingers and

stepped forward as a man about his age jumped out of the passenger seat. Framed by a fur-trimmed hood, his face creased in a wide smile as he spoke in accented English.

'Bianca Forrester and Xanthos Antoniou, I presume?' He grinned. 'We've been looking for you.'

CHAPTER FIVE

'I AM NOT doing this,' Xanthos stated, with grim emphasis. 'I am not sharing a room with you again, Bianca.'

Silently, Bianca counted to ten because Xanthos was being about as insulting as only he could be, but since she had already decided to rise above it, she adopted her most diplomatic tone. They had managed to survive almost twenty-four hours in a deserted mountain hut without killing each another—surely they could manage a few more? At least here there were other people around, so there would be something else to focus on other than the sexy Greek. 'I can assure you it isn't my idea of fun either, but—'

'But what?' he demanded, the sweeping movement of his arm drawing her attention to the snowy village square outside the window, where a giant conifer was decked with coloured lights. For a moment her imagination drifted away from her. She thought how pretty it looked in the moonlight and how sweet the little children seemed, who were gazing up in wonder at its sparkling branches.

'Why are we having to spend Christmas Eve in some godforsaken hotel in the middle of nowhere?' he continued, in that same harsh voice which completely broke the spell.

All her best conciliatory intentions forgotten, Bianca scowled. 'Will you please keep your voice down?' she hissed. 'I don't know how you can be so ungrateful. Especially as you treated me to a lecture on that very subject before you gave me a lift on your plane.'

'That's different.'

'How is it different? The most important thing is that we're safe, Xanthos. We were rescued, weren't we? By the village doctor, no less! We've been examined and given a clean bill of health and told that we can leave—'

'When?'

Bianca sucked in an unsteady breath. 'Dr Druri explained all that, too. You know he did. The road to the main airport is still partially blocked and it's not safe to attempt to get there tonight—but they've said it'll be okay tomorrow once the snow ploughs have been out. Plus, it's Christmas Eve and apparently that's a big deal in Vargmali. We were lucky to get the last room in the hotel *and* they've invited us to their big festive feast downstairs tonight.'

'I'm not interested in attending a festive feast,' he growled.

'Surely you're not so much of a Scrooge that you want to spoil everyone's fun?' she demanded. 'What else are we going to do— sit and stare at each other all evening and demand that an already overworked kitchen prepares something especially for us? That would be a big slap in the face for their hospitality, wouldn't it? At least up here we've got…' She let her words trail off, terrified that her forced her air of bravado would slip and she would give away the precarious state of her emotions. She wished she could wave a magic wand to transport her back to England—and yet the thought of having to say goodbye to this enigmatic man with whom she'd spent a night in a snowy mountain hut was bothering her far more than it should have done. 'Here we've got more than one place to sleep, so we won't have to share a bed,' she continued gamely. 'That fold-up divan over there looks comfortable enough.'

'You think so?' he questioned repressively. 'It looks more like a bed of nails to me.'

'Well, I don't mind sleeping on it, so that's settled.' She breathed out an unsteady sigh. 'I don't know why you can't just accept the situation we're in, Xanthos. You were the one who came out with all that stuff about accepting the things you can't control, which is exactly what I'm trying to do. What's the matter—is it really so awful, the thought of having to endure another night with me?'

Xanthos didn't reply immediately, mostly because he was still having difficulty getting his head around the fact that he remained trapped. With her. And there didn't seem to be a thing he could do about it. After a bumpy ride up the mountain road, to the accompanying chatter of the village doctor who had examined them both in his small surgery, they had arrived at this gothic monstrosity of a hotel, where he and Bianca had been shown into a large and rather draughty room.

After their snowy hut, the accommodation seemed almost luxurious—but continued proximity to a woman who was strictly off-limits was something he wanted to avoid at all costs. She was unsettling him, big-time, and he still couldn't work out why. The situation wasn't helped by the fact that everyone thought they were a couple and any attempts to dissuade them of this notion seemed to get lost in translation. Was that because when the search party had arrived, Bianca had been clinging to his arm, with him holding onto her as if she were a fragile piece of porcelain which might shatter if he let her go?

At least the hotel had a phone signal—of sorts—and on arrival he'd received a blitz of messages, most of which he'd ignored. His first priority had been to text Bianca's sister to reassure her she was safe, resisting the urge to comment that if she hadn't insisted on him giving her a ride in his plane, her anxious night of worrying could have been avoided.

And wouldn't you have found the experience much harder on your own? taunted a voice inside his head. *Didn't having Bianca Forrester there give you something to fight for?*

He had also received several texts from Kiki—her initial understanding about his emergency landing having morphed into a flurry of inappropriate questions about the nature of his relationship with his female passenger, because it seemed that the press had got hold of the story of their rescue and speculation was running rife. It struck him that the supermodel was behaving like some wounded lover when he barely knew her. But that, he reminded himself grimly, was women for you. You gave them the glimmer of an opening and, inevitably, they attempted to prise it apart.

And wasn't the truth that he *was* slightly obsessed by Bianca? He found himself plagued by a flurry of unwanted memories, which kept hitting him at the most inconvenient times. The shampoo scent of her hair and the sleepy brush of her lips against his jaw. The way her petite body had moulded so naturally into his. How easy it would have been to…

To…

But he mustn't think about that.

Why was he even thinking about her at all?

'Do you think there's any danger of getting a drink round here?' he growled.

'Why don't you go downstairs and investigate while I have a shower?' she suggested sweetly.

Xanthos left the room without another word, blotting out images of her standing in a steamy cubicle and lathering soap over those magnificent breasts. He made his way down the echoing flight of stairs to the hotel entrance, past several glass counters in the foyer which—bizarrely—were displaying root vegetables for sale. There was also a large Christmas tree—big and bushy and hung with rudimentary paper decorations which had obviously been crafted by children. Compared to its glitzy counterpart which sparkled outside the Rockefeller Center in his native New York every year, it was about as humble as you could get—yet there was something about the simple decorations which made him linger for a moment, before shaking his head with impatience and quickly walking away.

He passed a large dining room, in which several women were hanging swathes of festive greenery and chattering happily in their own language. The small bar was empty but eventually he found someone to serve him, then sat nursing a glass of malt whisky, until he heard the sound of people arriving in the main foyer, clearly in celebratory mood.

Finishing off the final mouthful, he made his way unenthusiastically back upstairs, wondering if he could plead a headache and spend the evening working, but these thoughts slid from his mind when he found Bianca dressed, her hair a glimmer of shiny waves set off dramatically by her black dress. Indignation vied with desire and indignation won. Wasn't it enough he had lain there like a rock during the long night when she had snuggled into his arms? Was she *trying* to test his resolve still further? To elevate his heart-rate to dangerous levels and make him ache for her with frustrated longing?

Steadying his suddenly erratic breathing, he tried telling himself that no way could her dress be described as provocative. Not when it was buttoned all the way down the front and hung in modest folds to her knees. So why this kick of lust so potent that it was making him unable to think about anything other than how much he wanted to touch her? Actually, he wanted to do a lot more than touch her. He wanted to be inside her. To shudder out his seed and fill her until he was empty and dry.

His body tensed.

Why the hell was he thinking like some kind of caveman?

'You don't like it?' she croaked.

Dragging himself out of his erotic daze, he stared at her uncomprehendingly. 'Don't like what?'

'My dress.' She shrugged. 'The way I look.'

'Why are you asking me that?'

'Because…' Bianca swallowed down the lump which had risen in her throat. His face had grown so incredibly *tense*. Golden olive skin was stretched taut over the high definition of cheekbones and his mouth had hardened into a forbidding slash. Her lawyerly articulation seemed to have deserted her in her time of need, as she struggled to find the right words. Or were they the wrong words? Wouldn't the wisest thing be to keep her mouth shut and not stray into the dangerous territory of the personal? But she couldn't seem to hold back her curiosity and, after the night they'd shared, surely she should be able to speak frankly to him. 'Because you're staring at me as if you couldn't…as if you've never seen me before. As if you don't know me.'

'Because I don't,' he asserted harshly into the brittle silence which followed. 'Just like you don't know me. And that's the way I would prefer it to stay, Bianca. We were trapped on a mountainside but it's over. We have a few more hours to get through and then we can go our separate ways and need never see one another again. So if you'll excuse me, I'll go and wash up.'

As the bathroom door closed behind him,

Bianca told herself he was rude and cold and positively obnoxious and she couldn't wait to be rid of him. Looking around for something to distract herself with, she picked up her phone to text her mother and sister again, this time to wish them a happy Christmas. And, even though she was on her honeymoon, Rosie's dramatic reply came winging straight back:

What do you think of Xanthos???!!!!

Bianca was certain her sister would derive little comfort from her opinion that she found him brave and strong and yet extremely hurtful. And that, bizarrely, she really wanted to have sex with him.

She kept her reply vague.

Very capable in an emergency! Enjoy your honeymoon. B xx

Putting the phone back down, she stared out of the window at the Christmas tree in the snowy village square below, thronging with people enjoying the festivities. Did children hang up stockings in Vargmali? she wondered, when the bathroom door opened and Xanthos walked into the room.

Perhaps if she had been prepared for his sudden appearance she might have been able to do something about her reaction but, as it was, she could do nothing to prevent the lurch of her heart or sudden shivering of her skin. He had changed into dark trousers and a pale silk shirt left open at the neck, revealing a tantalising triangle of gleaming skin. He looked utterly irresistible, she acknowledged reluctantly, every pore in her body unfurling into sensual life as he raked his fingers back through his still damp hair. Their eyes met. Their gazes held. She could almost *hear* the crackle of sex and danger in the air and suddenly she was glad they were going downstairs to eat—anywhere but staying up here, cocooned in this bedroom and susceptible to the ever-present temptation he represented.

'Ready?' she questioned briskly, with a quick glance at her watch. 'They said they're starting the meal at seven-thirty.'

'I can hardly wait.'

She turned to him. 'You're not going to be in a foul temper and ruin the night for everyone, are you?'

'No, Bianca. I give you my word. I will be diplomacy personified.'

'That will be a first.'

They made their way downstairs and as they entered the dining room and everyone looked up, Bianca suddenly realised that she felt like part of a couple—which had never happened before. Wasn't that a sad indication of how insular her life had become? At her all-girls school she'd worked hard to get the grades she needed and had kept to that same rigorous pattern all through uni. And yes, of course she had dated along the way, but no close bond had ever been formed. Her single-minded goal of independence had always seemed more important than being with a man.

But she could never remember feeling more *alive* than she did as Dr Druri's smiling young wife—who was called Ellen—handed them both some mulled wine and introduced them to the other guests. It was a mixed gathering and everyone was fizzing over with yuletide merriment. There were little children and teenagers. Long-married couples and a pair of newly-weds. A babe-in-arms and a very old man who lovingly kissed the forehead of his wife, as she sat in her wheelchair. Most people spoke a smattering of English but Bianca quickly realised the effectiveness of sign language and it transpired that Xanthos could speak fluent Italian, on which the Vargmalian language was based, so was able to give a succinct account of their plane crash.

She looked around the dining room, taking in the way it had been decorated—inexpensively but beautifully. In fact, she couldn't remember ever seeing anything quite so lovely and she whispered as much to Xanthos. Fragrant fresh greenery was looped around the window frames as well as along the top of the stone fireplace, where an enormous log fire crackled. More greenery was wreathed in startling contrast against a snowy-white tablecloth, where tall red candles lit the room with their golden and flickering glow. It was old-fashioned and simple. It was like Christmas was supposed to be and suddenly Bianca found herself overcome by a great yearning for…

What?

There was absolutely no evidence of luxury or vast amounts of money here. It was a world she didn't really recognise, yet somehow it felt real. More real than anything she could ever remember.

'Come and sit down!' exclaimed Ellen. 'Over here! Our guests of honour.'

Bianca slid into her seat as Xanthos took his place beside her and she turned to him. 'Isn't this wonderful?'

'Absolutely wonderful,' he murmured, and she prayed that nobody else had picked up on his sardonic undertone.

Course after course of delicious food arrived. Fish and pastries, berries and bonbons—all served on what was obviously the best china and accompanied by glasses of the rich local wine. Fortunately the chatter around the table was so voluble that nobody seemed to notice that she and Xanthos merely picked at their food, or if they did they were too polite to mention it.

When the feast was over and Bianca was wondering whether they should make their excuses and leave, the old man got up from the table and went to a corner of the room. Picking up his accordion, he started to play a tune which brought shouts of delighted recognition and, immediately, several people got up to dance.

'Dance with your wife, Xanthos!' urged Ellen encouragingly.

'She's not—'

'A very good dancer!' interjected Bianca hastily, jumping to her feet and smiling as she held out her hands to him. 'But who cares about that?'

Which left Xanthos with no choice other than to pull her into his arms—something which, contrarily, would have been at the very bottom and very top of his wish-list, at exactly the same time. 'Why the hell did you say that?' he growled, into her hair.

'Say what?'

'Implying we were married.'

'It just seemed easier,' she whispered back, her breath soft and warm against his ear. 'Relax, Xanthos. I'm not planning on frog-marching you up the aisle any time soon.'

He closed his eyes as the jaunty chords of the accordion echoed around the room and other couples swayed nearby and thought how good she felt as she moved against him. Indecently good. When had been the last time he had danced with a woman? He frowned. Had he *ever* danced with a woman? He didn't really *do* dancing, but maybe he'd been missing out for all these years. He could feel her breasts pushing into his chest, sending arrows of desire straight to his groin. 'Mmm…' he said, without thinking.

She drew back, her green eyes questioning. "'Mmm…" what?'

'I guess it's not so bad after all,' he conceded, as he whirled her around and he could hear the sound of her soft laughter beneath the notes of the accordion.

They danced until trays of sour-cherry drinks were handed around and the evening concluded with a group of children who arrived to entertain them with a medley of Vargmalian Christmas carols. A mixed clutch of pre-teens began to sing, including a boy whose voice hadn't broken—and whose delivery of the top notes sounded like an angel soaring through the now silent room. It was an emotionally charged moment and, as Xanthos observed wistfulness on the faces of the old and hope on the faces of the young, for the first time in his life he understood the appeal of Christmas.

But he understood too why he had always turned his back on it.

Then, and maybe now too.

'Let's go upstairs,' he said roughly, once the carols had finished, and he saw her nod, resignation darkening her eyes, as if she never wanted the evening to end.

'Okay,' she said.

As they said goodbye and mounted the stairs towards their room, Bianca knew she mustn't read too much into what had just happened. He had danced with her. And just because it had felt as heavenly as anything she could ever remember doing it didn't *mean* anything. It was Christmas, that was all—and Christmas was notorious for putting a dangerous spin on things. She knew she needed to cultivate a degree of impartiality before they spent their final night together, but as the door closed behind them all she could think about was how powerful and sexy he looked. The moonlight was splashing his dark hair with silver and making her want to run her fingers through those luxuriant metallic strands. She longed for the music of the accordion. She wanted to be back in his arms.

As he walked over to the window to stare out at the starry blaze of the Christmas tree in the village square, Bianca wanted to rail against the fact that he had managed to captivate her, despite all the defences she'd erected. That somehow he had made her want him, and that couldn't be allowed to continue. So why not defuse the situation? You've still got a whole night to get through. At least let him remember you as someone who knows her manners.

'I still haven't thanked you properly,' she said quietly.

He turned round. 'For what?'

'Oh, you know. For saving my life. For looking after me so well. For going back to the plane. For building a fire For...' She hesitated. 'Well, for behaving like such a gentleman.'

'Don't push it, Bianca.' His smile was wry, his words coated with something unfamiliar. 'Because I can assure you I'm not feeling in the least bit gentlemanly right now.'

Something in the way he was looking at her made rational thought drain from her mind, like the trickle of sand through open fingers. 'Oh?'

'Do you say "oh" like that because you know it makes your lips soften into the perfect pout?' he probed silkily. 'Meaning that I'm powerless to do anything except think about kissing you?'

'I can't imagine you ever being powerless, Xanthos.'

His mouth hardened. 'You'd be surprised.'

'Maybe I like surprises.'

But if she was expecting him to start confiding in her—to explain what had infused his words with that layer of bitterness—then she had misjudged him. Because clearly it wasn't understanding he sought. She could see from the blaze of his eyes that his needs were far more fundamental than that. Just like hers.

And suddenly she wanted her secret fantasy to take shape. She wanted him to pull her into his arms, only this time, not to dance. She wanted him to kiss her in this moon-washed room on the night before Christmas and take that kiss to its natural conclusion.

'I want you,' he stated softly.

'I didn't think I was your type.'

'I'm pretty sure you're not. But right now, that doesn't seem to matter.'

'Doesn't it?' she questioned, as if she had this kind of discussion every day. But although she'd never had sex before, she was certainly familiar with negotiation.

'Maybe it's that survival thing,' he continued, narrowing his dark eyes as he studied her. 'Needing to celebrate the life force when you've lived through the possibility of imminent death.'

'Is that what it is?' she said slowly, bitterly disappointed by his factual assessment.

Did he detect that his unsentimental words—although commendably honest—were threatening to undermine his ultimate goal? Was that why he walked over and touched his palm against her cheek, as if to frame it, or to revel in its softness? Or was he just clever enough to recognise that the romantic gesture was as seductive as the moonlight? To recognise that once he touched her she would be lost.

And she was.

Totally lost.

CHAPTER SIX

HE'D FANTASISED ABOUT kissing her lips for so long and now they were soft and trembling beneath his. Xanthos tangled his fingers into the soft, rich spill of Bianca's hair and as she brought her curvy hips in line with his, he groaned. Could she feel the imprint of his erection through the thin silk of her dress and did she find it daunting?

It would seem not, for she kissed him back with a hungry passion he hadn't been expecting from the cool and independent lawyer. And now she was circling those delicious hips against his legs and he was uncertain whether she was teasing him or testing him, and he drew back.

'You do know that if you don't slow down, this is all going to be over very quickly,' he warned her unsteadily.

He might have imagined her brief uncertainty, but he definitely didn't imagine her familiar challenge. 'And do you have a problem with that?'

He groaned again and his breath felt as if it were being ripped from the base of his lungs, because her provocative question appeared to give him permission to behave, not badly, no, but without any of the restraint he had been clinging onto since he'd landed that plane. Usually, he was the master of slow seduction and finesse. He always took his time. And in a way, didn't his protracted pleasuring of his lovers intensify his own satisfaction by demonstrating his steely self-control?

But there was very little self-control in his body now. Was it that ridiculously sentimental dance downstairs which had robbed him of sense and of reason? As he scooped Bianca into his arms and carried her towards the bed, he felt as if he were on fire. His kiss had never been so hot or hard or hungry, especially when he felt the imprint of a pair of hold-up stockings against his fingers. He toppled her down onto the bed and lay down beside her and his fingers were actually trembling as they began the interminable prospect of releasing the buttons of her dress. How many were there?

'I feel like ripping the damned thing off,' he growled.

'Rip away,' she invited insouciantly. 'There's plenty more clothes in my suitcase.'

And, God forgive him—but he did. With no regard whatsoever for the silky gown, he clasped the delicate fabric on either side of the buttons and wrenched it open. It came apart with a splitting sound, revealing her magnificent breasts—the globes encased in shadowy black lace, which were rising and falling in time with her rapid breathing.

'*Evge...*' he breathed, lapsing into a language he rarely spoke these days. His mouth twisted. His *mother* tongue. The word filled him with disdain, but his bitter contemplation dissolved the moment he bent his tongue towards the proud nipple which strained through the black lace, just begging to be licked. And when he obliged with the slow flick of his tongue, she squirmed her hips against the mattress with restless hunger and he felt himself grow even harder. His throat dried as he dealt with the skimpy lace panties—her open-thighed invitation consigning them to the same sorry fate as her ripped dress. His finger slid irresistibly over the slick heat at her core and, although he hadn't intended to, he began to stroke her until she was gasping and pleading with him.

'No,' he said, still filled with that delicious sense of the primal which was influencing his behaviour in the most uncharacteristic way. 'Not like that. Not the first time.'

'How many times are we going to do it?'

'That depends.'

'On what?'

'On this.' He kissed her some more, and then more still. She seemed unwilling to let him drag his mouth away from hers and he certainly wasn't objecting. At least, not until he thought he might explode if he didn't get inside her. Unzipping his trousers with difficulty, he hauled his shirt over his head until at last they were both naked and she was running her gaze over him with greedy fervour, almost as if she'd never seen a naked man before. But wasn't he doing exactly the same? Feasting his eyes on the black hold-up stockings which he had left in situ. Her hair was dark against the pillow and her teeth looked very white in the moonlight. As her gaze roved down to study his aching groin he thought he saw her bite her lip and wondered if she was reconsidering her options. Had she changed her mind?

And didn't some bone-deep instinct tell him it would be better for them both if she had, even though it would half kill him to walk away from her now? Because there was still her connection to his brother—the brother he had decided he was never going to see again.

'You want me to stop?' he questioned, through a throat so raw it felt as if someone were throttling him.

'Are you out of your mind?' she breathed, with a shake of her dark head. 'I want this, too, Xanthos. So badly.'

Her honesty was flattering and, again, surprising. In his experience, women usually held back their true feelings until they were hopeful they might be reciprocated. But Bianca Forrester had broken the mould. He frowned. Did she imagine this was going to end in a hail of confetti in County Hall, with flowers in her hair and a shiny gold band on her finger?

But maybe he was guilty of patronising her. She was a woman in her mid-twenties and a successful lawyer—not some guileless young innocent unused to the wicked ways of the world. They were stranded in an unknown country after sharing a dramatic experience, and then being shown the kindness of strangers on the most unashamedly emotional night of the year. What could be a more perfect ending to a roller coaster of a day and a lucky escape than a long night of delicious sex?

'You and me both. Very badly,' he echoed. The pragmatic interchange reminded him to get up and delve around in his suitcase, because he always used protection. He thought how wanton she looked, lying waiting for him in the moonlight, her black-stockinged legs bent and drawing him irrevocably towards her. He bent his head and kissed her until she was writhing with longing. 'You are exquisite,' he whispered.

'Am I?'

He could hear the uncertainty in her voice and that surprised him, too. 'Utterly.'

'Oh,' she breathed.

His fingertip lightly feathered the silken flesh at her thigh. 'Is that good?'

'You know it is,' she said thickly.

He licked her neck, her shoulders and her upper arms, tasting the salty perfume of her flesh. He licked the pouting tips of her breasts and took one into his mouth as he positioned himself over her, her warm thighs parting eagerly beneath his questing fingers. And when at last he pushed into her slick heat, it was…

He grew still.

Was it because he was so aroused that she felt so unbelievably *tight*?

'Bianca?' he ground out, every sinew in his body tensing with fierce control.

'Yes,' she whispered back.

But he heard the slight break underpinning her reply and knew instantly what had caused it.

'Bianca—'

'Please don't stop,' she urged him softly. 'Not now. Please keep doing exactly what you're doing.'

Stop? It would have been easier to command his own heart to cease beating, than to have held back from that next delicious thrust. 'You mean, like this?' he questioned unevenly.

'Y-yes. Ex-exactly like that,' Bianca whispered back as a wave of delicious heat flooded through her. And as he filled her, she couldn't hold back the thought that maybe she had been born to have Xanthos Antoniou inside her like this. Would it be insane to admit that somehow he made her feel complete, for the first time in her life? A sense of exhilaration accompanied her soaring joy as he thrust deeper inside her and, weirdly, she seemed to know exactly how to respond. It felt instinctive to wrap her legs around his back and tilt her hips to accommodate his hard rhythm. And didn't his ragged sighs of appreciation thrill her even more, letting her know how much she was pleasuring him? She had never felt so uninhibited, nor so in touch with a side of herself she'd always kept buried and, willingly, she let go. Of thought. Of control. Of everything. So free did she feel that her orgasm startled her. One minute she was opening her lips to the urgent plunge of his tongue and the next she was gasping as her body contracted ecstatically around him.

She could feel his urgency as he slid his palms beneath her buttocks, making those last few thrusts like a man possessed, before giving a shuddered moan which seemed to split the night. For a while he didn't move. He just stayed on top of her while the pulsing of his body grew quieter. Reaching down, he pushed a strand of hair away from her hot cheek, and though there was only moonlight to see by, it couldn't disguise the question in his narrowed gaze.

But Bianca didn't want to spoil what had

just happened with some forensic question-and-answer session about why he was the first. She didn't want him thinking it was anything more special than simple sexual chemistry.

Because it wasn't.

Willing the crashing of her heart to subside, she curved her lips into a smile and attempted to take charge of the conversation. To take back control. 'Wow,' she said softly. 'That was amazing.'

For a moment there was a silence punctured only by the sound of their laboured breathing.

'You know, I am rarely surprised by a woman, Bianca,' he said eventually. 'But it seems you have broken the mould.'

'Isn't Christmas supposed to be about surprises?' she questioned glibly.

But he didn't take the hint and shut up.

'You certainly are a total mind-blowing contradiction to the woman you appear to be,' he mused. 'An apparently sophisticated career woman in her mid-twenties, who sends out the very definite message that she's modern and liberal—who turns out to be a blushing virgin.'

She huffed out a sigh and, despite her best

endeavours, started wondering whether some kind of explanation was inevitable. Maybe it was, but she made one last attempt to deflect it. 'I don't remember blushing.'

'You certainly are now,' he offered drily.

She ran her fingertip over the outline of his lips. 'Please don't worry about me, Xanthos. I am as modern and as liberal as they come–'

'And you certainly did come,' he observed.

'I'm just not very experienced, that's all.'

'I think I managed to work that one out for myself.' There was a pause. 'And I'm wondering what the reason is. You're under no obligation to tell me, of course.'

Bianca hesitated. Why *not* tell him the truth—especially if this relationship was going to go anywhere? 'I've never really had time for men, that's why,' she admitted slowly. 'I've spent most of my life working very hard to make something of myself—'

'Even though you grew up in the grounds of an actual palace?'

'Why do people always jump to the same conclusion? The palace was like living in a very fancy rented house! Honestly. We had no real money of our own. Everything we did was dependent on what the King wanted and I knew I didn't want to live like that. That whatever I wanted to achieve, I was going to have to do without any outside help from anybody else.' Now it was her turn to study him questioningly. 'Could you honestly say the same, Xanthos?'

'You think I was born with a silver spoon in my mouth?'

She shrugged. 'I don't know. To be honest, I don't really know anything about you. Were you?'

Xanthos looked out of the window at the snowy rooftops of Vargmali, recognising that it would be the easiest thing in the world to clam up. To shut down her questions about his formative years with a kiss, because that was what he always did. But on this strange Christmas Eve in this faraway land, the normal rules didn't seem to apply. They had been thrown together in more ways than one and the bizarre sequence of events had an air of impermanence about it, like the tall tree which glittered in the village square, which would be taken down before the new year was very old.

And maybe his uncharacteristic introspection had something to do with seeing his brother again—because hadn't that thrown up the kind of questions he would usually have buried? Wasn't it inevitable he should have started comparing Corso's upbringing to his—and to have been reminded just how grim his own had been? It would be a mistake to reveal too much of himself to Bianca, of all people—yet his need to talk to someone was stronger than it had ever been. And lawyers were trained to be discreet, weren't they? So maybe he would give her some of the facts. Just not all of them. Especially not the ones which impacted on her own sister.

'My mother got married very young when she discovered she was pregnant,' he said. 'And for the first sixteen years of my life I knew wealth on a scale which most people can barely imagine.'

He waited for her to come back at him with a triumphant retort. To say something like, 'So you *were* rich!' But she didn't.

'And was it a happy childhood?'

'Is there such a thing?' he questioned bitterly.

'Wow.' The single word was soft. 'That's a very cynical thing to say, Xanthos. Cryptic, too.'

'It might be—but that's the way I think. It's one of the reasons I don't intend having any children of my own.'

She nodded at this, as if storing away the knowledge so she could take it out and look at it later. 'So it wasn't happy?'

No need to document the gnawing acknowledgement that there had always been a strange kind of tension around his parents. He'd thought it inevitable, given the huge and often embarrassing age gap. He didn't mention the way his father used to look at him sometimes—as if he had crawled out from beneath a stone. His mother had looked at him that way too sometimes, hadn't she? And somehow that had been much, much worse.

'Oh, I wasn't beaten or starved,' he said flippantly. 'But on my sixteenth birthday, my father decided to give me a highly unconventional present.'

'Not a car, then?'

'No, nor a watch. He decided I needed a DNA test.' He paused. 'So a doctor came to the house to take blood.'

He saw the consternation which creased her face. 'But…why?'

'You're an intelligent woman, Bianca,' he prompted silkily. 'Why do you think?'

'He suspected he wasn't your father?'

'Indeed he did.' His jaw hardened as he

gritted his teeth. 'And he was right. Because he wasn't.'

'Oh, my goodness,' she breathed. 'How difficult must that have been? What…what happened?'

Xanthos shifted his position on the bed, his gaze lifting to the silvery moon outside the window as he wondered what was happening to him. Why were all the defences with which he had surrounded himself for as long as he could remember, now threatening to crumble? And even though an insistent voice in his head was urging him to shut down the conversation, he found himself wanting to break the rule of a lifetime and tell her, because he'd never admitted this, not to anyone. 'What happened was that he gave my mother an ultimatum. He said it was either him, or me. She could stay, but only if I went.'

She gave a slightly nervous laugh. 'But she chose you, right?'

Xanthos could feel his throat constrict because this was the hardest part of all, even now. *This* was the reason he had locked it away. *This* was the shameful part. Because a mother who rejected her only child…

Had he really been that unlovable?

But it was good to remember these things,

no matter how painful it might be. It helped him put things in perspective. It stopped him from painting reality with unrealistic shades of longing. It reinforced his certain knowledge that there was no such thing as love.

'Wrong,' he corrected caustically. 'She figured that, of the two of us, I stood a better chance of survival on my own than she did—since she was totally dependent on her husband financially and had no money of her own. So I was kicked out of the house and told to fend for myself.'

She turned onto her side, propping herself up on her elbow so that a stream of dark waves tumbled over her bare breasts. 'How did you survive?'

He shrugged. 'I already attended a very prestigious school in New York City who were reluctant to see me go, though it wasn't unusual for boys to have to leave the school due to reduced circumstances. But they arranged for me to take a scholarship exam and I ended up staying there as a boarding-school pupil.'

She twirled the end of a strand of hair round and round her finger. 'But what about school holidays?'

'I had some very wealthy friends and one

in particular. His name was Brad Wilson and I used to stay with him and his family.' But Xanthos had been a cold, proud youth, suspicious of kindness—mainly because he had experienced so little of it. Hadn't his willingness to accept what he perceived as charity from the Wilsons been because their East Side reserve had meant they never asked him any painful and personal questions? And hadn't one of the principal reasons they had taken him into their family been because he *hadn't* emoted?

'And was that…okay?'

He thought about it. *Okay* seemed a pretty accurate description of a period of his life at that time—because he had been obsessed with his own independence and wondering when he would be able to gain it. 'I was grateful to them,' he said at last. 'But it reinforced my belief that family life is claustrophobic. Soon after that I went to Stanford to do computer science and dropped out after two years to start my video gaming company.'

'And do you still see Brad?' she said slowly, as if it mattered.

It was a curveball of a question and the punch of pain was unexpected. It reminded him of why he functioned best when he avoided any kind of emotional attachment. 'That would be impossible, I'm afraid,' he said slowly. 'He and his father died in a boating accident soon after he left college. His mother never really recovered from the blow, and she died within the year. Within the space of eighteen months, they were all wiped out. Gone.'

Bianca saw the sudden tension in his face as he lapsed into an uneasy silence. She was deeply moved and taken aback by what he had told her, which just went to show that you never knew what anybody was really like on the inside. Who would have thought the outrageously sexy billionaire should have had such a tragic upbringing? That he should have endured so much pain and sorrow, as well as a mother who had chosen her husband over her only son. Couldn't he be forgiven some of his harsh arrogance in the light of this new knowledge?

'And did you ever ask your mother who your real father was?'

'No.'

Something about the flat delivery of his reply made her ask her next question. 'Do you still see her?'

'I haven't seen her since that day she kicked me out. I have no idea where she lives.'

'And don't you…?' She hesitated, recognising that this might be overstepping the mark. 'Don't you think maybe you should try to find her?'

'Why the hell should I do that?' he demanded.

She shrugged. 'It might help you move on, if you could see her again, understand her perspective more.'

'No.' The single word was clipped out like a bullet and as his features became cold, he looked so different from the man who had taken her into his arms and told her how much he wanted to kiss her. Was it that which made her reach out to frame his cheek with her palm, mirroring what he'd done to her just before they'd had sex? She thought how wonderful his lovemaking had been. How he had managed to help create the most magical Christmas Eve she could remember and made her feel properly alive for the first time in her life. She didn't want the night to end with him looking angry and bitter as he recalled the acrimony of his past. She wanted to hear him moan with pleasure again.

Tentatively she let her thumb rove over

the strong curve of his jaw and he stirred in response, the stoniness leaving his face and making it flesh again. His eyes gleamed with sudden fire—as if he had just remembered there was a naked woman in his bed. And maybe he was as loath to miss this opportunity as she was, for he pulled her into his arms, bringing her to lie on top of him.

'I don't want to talk about it any more,' he gritted out.

'I sort of guessed that for myself,' she whispered back.

'In fact, talking is the last thing on my mind right now.'

And Bianca nodded, because she was right there with him. All she cared about was the hardness nudging so insistently against her thighs and the answering rush of heat as her hungry lips sought his.

CHAPTER SEVEN

'WE WILL SHORTLY be coming in to land in London. The captain hopes you have both enjoyed a pleasant flight.'

The flight attendant's smile was wide, and the glass of wine she had recently served had been cold and delicious, but Bianca's heart was pounding with anxiety as the plane began its descent through the wintry bleakness of the English morning sky. Everything was happening so fast that it felt like being on a non-stop merry-go-round and she thought, not for the first time, that this was turning out to be the most bizarre Christmas morning of her life.

Opposite her sat Xanthos, his long-legged frame reclining in the leather seat of the private jet he'd hired to fly them from Vargmali where, earlier today, they had left the tiny village of Kopshtell. With the Christmas bells peeling in their ears and big fat flakes of snow beginning to fall, many of the friendly villagers they'd met last night had turned up to wave them off. Bianca's heart had leapt as she had hugged Ellen and promised that they might try to come back one day. Had it been presumptuous of her to include Xanthos in her impulsive declaration to the local doctor's wife? Was that why he had been so *distant* towards her during the two-hour flight back to London?

After a long night of rapturous lovemaking when she had thought they were as close as two people could be, she had been given a short, sharp shock this morning. Because once they had dragged themselves from their rumpled bed at a hellishly early hour, there had been no touching, or complicit eye contact—no physical contact at all. For a start, Xanthos had dressed in an immaculate city suit and silk tie and that too seemed to set him apart since her own outfit was decidedly casual. Then he'd spent the entire journey working, giving no hint to the crew—or even to her—that they had been lovers. Looking at their body language, no one would have guessed that he had introduced her to pleasure after pleasure, or confided some pretty disturbing things about his childhood before clamming up completely—confidences she suspected were rare. Was he now regretting having made such frank disclosures to a woman who was little more than a stranger?

Consequently, Bianca now felt exhausted and oversensitive and wished she were back in that rural hotel. Somehow she had felt safe in that snowy village, high in the Vargmalian mountains—as if the normal cares of the world couldn't touch her there. She wondered what was going to happen between them now. If anything. What did she know? Had it just been a casual hook-up for him? Was she supposed to act as if nothing had happened? But if their passionate night *was* to be a one-off, she would accept it. She wouldn't chase him, or beg him or behave as if she was in any way *dependent* on him. Because she wasn't. She wasn't dependent on anyone.

She was just leaning forward to watch the green fields of England growing ever closer, when Xanthos's gravelled voice broke into her thoughts.

'So, what are you planning on doing when we touch down?'

Bianca turned to look at him, steeling herself against all his dark and golden beauty.

That didn't sound very promising, did it? 'I told you.' She tried to inject a note of enthusiasm into her voice as she thought of going home to her silent Wimbledon apartment. 'I'm just going to have a quiet Christmas Day on my own.'

Dark eyebrows disappeared into the ebony tumble of his hair. 'And is that what you really want?'

Of course it isn't what I want, you stupid man! I want you to pull me in your arms and tell me I'm beautiful and then kiss me, the way you did last night.

She experimented with a little cool flirtation. 'Why, is there an alternative?'

'I'm staying at the Granchester. I've booked a suite.'

He said it as if she would have heard of it—which of course she had. 'Just like that?' She blinked. 'One of the best hotels in London and you just happened to be able to get a suite there, on Christmas Day?'

He shrugged, drawing her unwilling attention to the broad width of his shoulders. 'The owner is a friend of mine.'

Of course he was. 'I thought…' She fiddled unnecessarily with her seat belt. 'I thought you were going to Switzerland.'

'I was, but I've altered my plans. I'm staying in London for a couple of days.' He subjected her to a steady gaze. 'And I thought you might like to join me.'

'Right.' She sat very still as those dark eyes washed over her. If she were here in a professional capacity she might have asked him why he had changed his plans, and her tone would have been crisp and direct and confident. But she wasn't here in a professional capacity. She was here as a woman who'd spent the previous night having sex and she wasn't sure how to handle the aftermath. What to say or how to react. If there were games people played after being intimate for the first time, nobody had ever told her the rules. Part of her wanted to fling herself into his arms and cover his face with kisses which although last night would have been welcomed, today she suspected would not. As always when she was uncertain, she sought comfort in procrastination. 'Let me think about it.'

Xanthos nodded, not sure whether to be amused or insulted by her lukewarm response, because his head was still all over the place. His night with Bianca had turned out to be the hottest of his life, even before he had made the astonishing discovery that she'd been a virgin. But even more surpris-ing than that was the fact that he had *told* her stuff. Stuff buried deep which never usually saw the light of day, because he wasn't a man given to introspection.

But she needed to understand this wasn't going anywhere. She still didn't know who he really was, and there were all kinds of rea-sons why that shouldn't change. If she knew, it would alter everything. For both of them. He just wasn't willing to let her go...not just yet. And didn't he have the perfect excuse for suggesting they prolong their liaison—one which wouldn't fill her with false hope about the future? He gathered up the documents he'd been reading during the flight. 'My of-fice have been in touch while we've been in the air. Apparently journalists are waiting for us to land.'

She looked at him blankly. 'Journalists?'

'You know. They usually write or broad-cast features of interest to the general public.'

'Very funny. Why would they do that? Be waiting for us, I mean.'

She pursed her soft lips and he was mo-mentarily distracted by the memory of those lips locked around a very intimate part of his anatomy, which had started to ache with unbearable precision. 'Think about it,' he said huskily. 'Your sister is a newly crowned queen, and I'm not exactly unknown in the world of gaming and finance. Our plane recently crashed in the snowy mountains of a distant country and we were rescued by a village doctor in an ancient truck. We spent the night together in a quirky hotel, and I'm afraid that being rich and single inevitably gives rise to speculation about the women in my life. It is also Christmas Day, which is a light news day.' He fixed her with a mocking look. 'Doesn't that give you a hint about why they might want to talk to us?'

'Well, I'm not talking to anyone!'

'Neither am I. Which is why I've arranged for a car to drive me straight from the airfield into London. Have you thought about it for long enough, Bianca?' His raised his eyebrows. 'You could join me at the Granchester and we could spend Christmas Day and night together, or I can drop you off somewhere else on the way.' He shrugged. 'Up to you.'

Bianca was tempted to turn him down because his attitude was so...*offhand*. As if she meant nothing to him, and the occasional tenderness she'd glimpsed when they'd been in bed had been nothing but a figment of her imagination. Or maybe tenderness was acceptable within the shadows of the night, but vanished when it met the cold scrutiny of daylight. Couldn't he at least have kissed her and pulled her into his arms and told her that he really, really wanted her to spend some time with him? He was being so...*cool.*

She stared down at her fingernails. She knew you weren't supposed to let other people's moods affect the way you felt, but right now that didn't seem to make any difference. She felt like a balloon which had been lanced by a needle. And although it was tempting to want to extend her time with him—wouldn't that be dicing with danger where her emotions were concerned?

But a solo Christmas dinner had definitely lost its appeal and the thought of returning to her small apartment made her feel flat. She pushed at one of her cuticles. Her seduction last night had felt inevitable—as if she would never stop regretting it if she said no. This one felt more considered and the decision was all hers. She knew what would be the right thing to do. To thank him for the memory and say goodbye, thus eliminating the chances of getting her heart broken. Yet hadn't she spent her whole life trying to do the right thing? She had adopted different roles when her father had become ill and her mother had found it so difficult to cope. She'd been hard-working Bianca. Reliable Bianca. But now she'd discovered passionate Bianca, surely she was allowed to savour that side of her personality before normal, sensible service was resumed.

'I suppose I could spend Christmas Day with you,' she said, after much deliberation. 'At least it'll save me from having to do any cooking. Or washing up.'

He smiled and Bianca felt vindicated in her decision when she saw the rabble of press in the distance as they descended the aircraft steps. The waiting car felt like a haven, though she was half blinded by the flash of cameras as they were driven at speed towards the exit. Leaning back, she expelled a long sigh of relief.

'Thank heavens that's over.'

His gaze was curious. 'Had many dealings with the press before?'

She shook her head. 'Not really. I had to refuse a couple of magazine interviews when the engagement was first announced, and shortly before the wedding I was papped leaving a corner shop near where I live in London after buying a carton of milk.' She pulled a face. 'It was an extremely unflattering photo, leaving them to speculate what on earth I was going to wear at the wedding which wouldn't make me look like a gatecrasher.'

'And did that bother you?'

'It did, because that kind of scrutiny was totally unexpected,' she answered slowly. 'From being a fairly anonymous person, I was slightly alarmed to discover that Rosie's new-found fame seemed contagious.'

There was a pause. 'And did you approve of your sister marrying the King?'

She tilted her head consideringly. He really could be quite surprising. At times he was insultingly offhand, while at others he did seem genuinely interested in her life, and her past. She shrugged. 'I didn't always like Corso, no.'

'Oh? Why not?'

The purring consideration of his question was at odds with the sudden tension which had invaded his body and Bianca wondered what had caused it. Was it simply a competitive aspect of his own character—that of one exceedingly successful man curious to hear about the defects of another? But he had confided in her last night, and surely she must trust herself to do the same. 'I thought he was arrogant,' she confessed. 'And that he would probably break her heart.'

'Because?'

'Because he's a rich royal who's had countless lovers in the past and Rosie has always been fairly naïve and was probably completely out of her depth.'

'But it all ended happily ever after?'

'Yes, it did. The power of love, I guess,' she added, unable to keep the curl of wistfulness from her voice.

He screwed his brow up as if she had just uttered some kind of profanity. 'You don't honestly believe in all that stuff?'

Bianca hesitated. She knew it wasn't cool to admit it, but something made her want to tell him the truth. Was it to ensure that he knew exactly where he stood with her? To warn him—or maybe to issue a silent plea—not to mess around with her own, innocent heart? 'I do, yes,' she said quietly. 'My mother and father loved one another very much and things were great between them until my father had his accident. But they provided a loving home for me and Rosie and I'd like…well, one day I'd like to recreate that sort of family life for myself, if I ever meet the right man.'

'Bianca—'

'Oh, please don't worry,' she said quickly, anticipating his words. 'I'm not including you in that consideration, Xanthos. I want someone, yes, but a nice safe man who doesn't make waves—who also wants a family of his own. And you're the antithesis of that man. The wrong man, if you like. Please don't be offended.'

'Why would I be offended when it's nothing but the truth? To be honest, it's a relief to hear you say it. Marriage has never been on my agenda and love is just a word which gets misused all the time. Whereas to be acknowledged as something of a scoundrel, which is what you seem to be doing, well, that's a much better fit.' He gave a dangerously sexy smile, his voice dipping into a velvety caress. 'Do you have any idea of how much I want you right now, Bianca?'

Her throat constricted. 'Maybe.'

'So what are we going to do about it?'

'You tell me,' she whispered. 'You're the expert.'

'Yes, but…'

She could see him swallow as he unbuttoned her jacket, cupping her breast through the thick wool of her sweater and caressing the covered nipple until it peaked against his palm.

'But, what?' she prompted.

'Right now you're making me feel like a novice,' he admitted huskily.

Was that good or bad? Bianca wondered as his hand continued to work its provocative magic. But by then he had turned his attention to the other breast and her head was tipping back helplessly against the squashy leather of the car seat. She could feel the tiptoeing of his fingers moving slowly up towards her thigh and as she felt irresistible hunger spiralling up, she managed to prise a splinter of logic from the befuddled depths of her mind, because surely she ought to stop him. 'What about…the driver?' she breathed weakly.

'Don't worry. He can't see us.' His lips began to brush along her jaw and she could feel the warmth of his quickened breath against her skin. 'Or hear us.'

'Are you…sure?'

'I'm certain. Total privacy is always a non-negotiable whenever I get a chauffeured car.'

She wished he hadn't said that because it conjured up pictures of other women who had been in exactly this situation. But she did nothing to stop the automatic parting of her thighs, nor the questing forefinger which had alighted with aching precision over the denim seam covering the crotch of her jeans. Her throat dried. 'Xanthos,' she breathed, her bottom writhing with frustration as he began to stroke her through the thick material.

'Xanthos, what?' he questioned, the mocking caress of his words turning her on even more.

She wanted to beg him to unzip her jeans and touch her properly. To place his finger against the bare flesh, or even use his mouth—as he had done so shockingly and so beautifully last night. But she was powerless to speak. Powerless to do anything other than try to contain her moans of pleasure as he took her to that exquisite place again.

She came quickly, almost violently, shuddering against his hand, her body clenching with sweet spasms as his head swooped down to claim her lips in a kiss. Blindly, she groped for the hard ridge in his trousers, but he bucked away as if she had scalded him, capturing her wrist within the curl of his fingers, his lips pressed close against her ear.

'No. Not now and not here,' he warned softly.

The spasms of her own pleasure still receding and aware that she was probably never going to get another sexual education like this, Bianca plucked up the courage to ask him directly. 'You mean, you don't want me to?' she questioned, unable to keep the confusion from her voice, and the silence which followed seemed to go on and on.

'More than you will ever know,' he answered in a strained kind of voice, before leaning back in his seat and straightening his silk tie. 'But I've always found deprivation to be good for the soul. Particularly when—'

'When, what?' she prompted.

But he shook his dark head with an air of finality, as if he'd already said too much. As if he wanted to distance himself from her both mentally and physically. Why else would he slide to the far end of the seat as the car drew up outside the Granchester and the liveried doorman sprang to attention?

CHAPTER EIGHT

THE CHRISTMAS TREE which dominated the atrium of the luxurious Granchester was enormous and Bianca gazed up at its laden branches, blinking her eyes against its bright shimmer. The fragrant fir was decked with expensive lights and baubles and, according to the breathless commentary from the concierge who was showing them around, the tiny pink glass pomegranates were a nod to Zac Constantinides, the hotel's Greek owner.

But all she could feel as she gazed up at its splendour was an aching sense of something which felt like *disappointment*. As if recognising that nothing could be as magical as the beauty of the simple tree they'd left behind in Kopshtell.

Her heart was racing and her skin glowing as a result of Xanthos bringing her to that shattering orgasm in the back of the luxury car just now, but it had been curiously a one-sided experience. He hadn't allowed her to touch him back and his expert ministrations had been delivered with the impartiality of someone who'd been following an instruction manual. It hadn't felt as if he were *involved*.

But then he wasn't involved, was he? Not really. From the moment they'd left the airfield, he'd shown her a completely different side to his character. He was no longer the man who had whirled her breathlessly around the dance floor last night, but a powerful and sophisticated entrepreneur with untold wealth at his fingertips. From the moment they'd walked into the Granchester people had been practically falling over themselves to talk to him. And he was used to that. She could tell. Suddenly, his exalted status had become very apparent.

She was quiet as they rode the private elevator to their vast suite, with its floor-to-ceiling windows and glittering chandeliers.

'Isn't this an improvement on what we've left behind?' he said, tugging off her coat and placing it on one of the giant leather sofas.

Bianca shrugged because her world had started to feel curiously disjointed. Here she was surrounded by nothing but opulence but all she wanted was to be back in that rustic hotel or even the snowy mountain hut, where their needs had been so basic and yet everything had seemed uncomplicated.

'I suppose so.'

He raised his eyebrows. 'You don't sound very enthusiastic.'

She shrugged. 'I liked it in Vargmali.'

'Then let's see what we can do to make you like it here, shall we?'

He unzipped her jeans and peeled away her sweater—his economy of movement belying the slight unsteadiness of his hands. Very soon she was lying unselfconsciously on a giant sofa in just her bra and panties and he was walking towards her, stripping off his clothes and letting them fall. His body was clearly aroused—but the shuttered expression on his face was unreadable and she wondered if she had imagined that warmer version of him yesterday, or whether the mountain air had briefly gone to his head. She lay back against the heap of silken cushions as his suit trousers hit the silken rug and tried to focus on the moment. She could see the unashamed power of his erection and acknowledged, with a touch of incredulity, how amazing it was that her body could accommodate something as big as that. The perfect fit. Like Cinderella's slipper, she thought dreamily as he grew closer.

'Please don't look at me like that,' he instructed unevenly.

'Like what?'

Xanthos felt his throat tighten even more. Like she wanted to devour him. Or bewitch him. Or to suck him deep inside her body and never let him go. But she had already done that, he reminded himself. She had offered him her virginity while he, in turn, had told her things he'd never told another soul. How much more of himself was he going to give this woman, and how much more of himself did he wish to expose? He needed to be in control, he reminded himself grimly—not relinquish any more of it to her, because of this strange physical alchemy they shared. 'It doesn't matter,' he said abruptly. 'Move over.'

She made room for him on the giant sofa and he distracted his wayward thoughts by removing her bra and her panties as slowly as possible—as if to demonstrate that not all his self-restraint had left him. Yet he couldn't prevent himself from drinking in her nakedness as she lay there, as if he were seeing her properly for the first time. And maybe he was. In the hut, the temperature had been icy, their thick layers of clothing vital in helping keep them alive. Even in the rural hotel, the air had been draughty enough to make them snuggle beneath the old-fashioned eiderdown. But here in the centrally heated luxury of the Granchester, he was able to feast his eyes on her body for the first time.

And she was *incredible*. Tiny and soft, her shape was curvy yet compact. Creamy breasts were crowned with nipples the colour of damask roses, and between her thighs a triangle of dark hair, which shielded the honeyed mound he had licked with such intensity. Caressing one lush breast between his fingers for an exquisitely long moment, he watched her emerald eyes darken and her hips wriggle with unconscious invitation.

'I can hardly believe you were a virgin,' he confessed slowly as he continued to stroke her.

The tip of her tongue roved over the cushion of her bottom lip and he wondered if she had any idea how provocative that was.

'Because…because I wasn't very good at it?' she ventured.

'It?' he mocked.

'Sex,' she elaborated shyly.

Shaking his head, he moved his hand down between her legs and felt her squirm with pleasure as he encountered her sticky heat. 'On the contrary,' he murmured, his finger moving lightly against her responsive flesh. 'You behaved as if you were born to it.'

'I suppose everyone is, when you think about it,' she answered, quite seriously, though the stilted delivery of her words suggested she was having difficulty concentrating when he was rubbing his finger against her like that. 'Otherwise, how would the human race ever have survived?'

His response was a short and surprising laugh. For a woman to amuse him was rare enough, but to do so when he was just about to have sex with her was unheard of. 'Tell me what you like best about it, so far,' he questioned, with a sudden indulgence.

'Everything. I like everything.'

Her eyelids had fluttered to a close and Xanthos was relieved, because that had sounded too much like unconditional praise for his liking. He hoped she wasn't going to start *caring* for him, and not just because she was the sister-in-law of his royal brother.

He stared at her flushed flesh. Yes, their bodies had met and matched with mind-blowing chemistry, but that was only one side of intimacy. Emotionally, she would be out of her depth and liable to mistake physical satisfaction for something else. Because that was what women did. It was how they operated. They attached emotions to actions which were never intended to be anything more than actions.

'In that case, let me show you some more of my repertoire,' he suggested on a silken boast.

'You're making it sound like performance art,' she grumbled.

'All life is performance.'

Bianca might have been tempted to continue the debate if he hadn't started kissing her and before too long he was easing himself into her body again and making her concerns vanish like dust on the wind.

Some time later, she went into one of the bathrooms and stood beneath a torrent of hot water and when she emerged, wrapped in a white robe, she realised that Xanthos must have used another of the bathrooms for he sat in a matching robe at a linen-draped table, which had been set up in front of the tall windows, overlooking the park. He was looking at something on his phone as she walked in, and if she was a little disappointed that he hadn't joined her in the shower she was sensible enough to keep her complaint to herself.

He put the phone down, but she noticed it was screen-side up.

'I've ordered us a very late lunch,' he said. 'Come and sit down.'

Obediently, she slid into the chair opposite, but she must have been hungrier than she'd anticipated for she tucked into lobster and a feta and spinach pastry, which was one of the most delicious things she'd ever eaten. It was certainly an unconventional Christmas dinner. There were grapes the colour of rubies, accompanied by slivers of French cheese, followed by stewed plums and thick, clotted cream. They drank iced water and, afterwards, champagne—served in faceted crystal flutes which sparkled like diamonds.

'This time it doesn't taste of toothpaste,' Xanthos observed wryly.

Bianca nodded but put the glass down after one sip, for the wine was making her feel vulnerable. Because wasn't the recollection of memories dangerous? Didn't it have the potential to create the idea that they shared some sort of history when they were just two people who had found themselves in an extraordinary situation and allowed sexual attraction to take over?

It made her realise just how quickly things had happened.

Too quickly.

'Is the owner of this hotel really a friend of yours?' she asked, deliberately redirecting her thoughts as she glanced out at London's famous Hyde Park.

'Zac?' Xanthos took a sip of his drink. 'We knew each other way back and our paths have crossed from time to time. In fact, you'll meet him later.' There was a pause. 'If you'd like to.'

She looked at him blankly. 'You mean, he's here? In the hotel?'

'Not right now. He and his wife live in Hampstead, but apparently it's a tradition to bring their children to see the Granchester tree on Christmas afternoon. He said it would be good to catch up as we haven't seen each other in a while, and I saw no reason to say no.'

She put her napkin down and gave a hesitant smile. 'Yes. Yes, I'd like that.'

'Good.' His dark eyes glittered with obsidian fire. 'But first I think you need to wipe that faintly concerned expression off your face and come over here so that I can kiss you.'

'Or you could come over here?'

'I could. But in order to do that I'd have to move.' His tone was dry as he directed a wry glance at his lap. 'And right now, I'm not sure I'd be able to.'

Bianca flushed with instinctive pleasure at the erotic inference and did as he asked, unsurprised when he untied her robe and placed his lips against her peaking nipple, and she gave a small moan of pleasure as his hardness sprang against her hungry fingers. The outcome was predictable, yet as Bianca began to rock back and forth on his rocky shaft, it felt as intense as the first time they'd made love. It was blissful when he closed his eyes like that and bit out a whimper of pleasure which sounded almost helpless. It gave her a heady rush of triumph which briefly obliterated all her doubts and uncertainties.

Nonetheless, she felt the skittering of nerves as she extricated herself from his embrace and hunted around for something suitable to wear, wondering what Xanthos's friends would think of her. Had they met many of his lovers in the past? Pulling out a short dress in festive scarlet, she held it up in

front of her, hoping the couple were sophisticated enough to be polite, even if they didn't
automatically approve of her.

But it seemed her fears were unfounded because handsome Zac and his blonde English
wife, Emma, were delightful. As were their
two children—Leo, a solemn, dark-eyed little boy of five, along with Eva, his thirteen
month-old baby sister, who was the spitting
image of her mother. The baby took an instant
shine to Bianca and, in particular, her long
hair—clamping a tight fist around one of the
long black waves and refusing to let go, no
matter how much her protesting mother tried
to disengage the little fingers.

'Honestly, I don't mind,' said Bianca, with
a smile. 'Though it might make it easier if I
held her?'

'You could *try*, though she probably won't
go to you,' said Emma doubtfully, bursting
into a peal of laughter as Eva immediately
launched herself into Bianca's arms. 'Oh, it
seems she will.'

It was a different kind of assault to the
senses from the ones she'd been experiencing
of late but as Bianca breathed in Eva's clean,
baby scent and a pair of chubby arms were
draped around her neck, she was overcome

by a wave of longing so powerful it felt almost visceral. A thought crossed her mind so quickly it was barely there, but it left an imprint as deep as if it had been branded there.

Will I ever hold a baby of my own like this?

As she pressed her chin against Eva's head, she met the ebony slice of Xanthos's gaze over the softly tousled curls and a pang of something unknown tugged painfully inside her. Was that a warning she had read in his eyes? With an unexpectedly heavy heart, she handed the baby back to Emma and prepared to accompany the Constantinides family into the main lobby.

Most of the Granchester staff were lined up on either side of the Christmas tree to welcome their boss, and a teddy bear and toy drum were produced for Eva and Leo, to delighted squeals. Afterwards, they went to the hotel's famous Garden Room, where tea was served. The courtyard outside was lit with hundreds of white lights, and tiny silvery stars were laced through the bare branches of the trees. In a far corner of the restaurant was a miniature battery-operated ice rink, on which tiny skaters in festive clothes of green and red whirled round and round. The two men took the children over for a closer look, while Bianca and Emma surveyed the glut of Christmas fare piled on the table with slight dismay, before ordering nothing stronger than ginger tea.

'You have two very beautiful children,' Bianca commented as the two women sat down.

Emma smiled. 'They like you. You're obviously a natural.' Her voice was soft but when Bianca didn't answer the unspoken question, she carried on speaking. 'I gather you've just come through a pretty horrendous experience.'

Bianca nodded, because she could hardly confess that what had happened subsequently had been enough to erase the plane crash from her mind. 'Yes, it was.' She hesitated. 'But Xanthos was absolutely amazing. I don't know whether anyone else would have coped as well as he did.'

'Mmm… I imagine he'd be a good person to have around in an emergency.' Emma's expression grew curious. 'He said he met you in Monterosso, at your sister's wedding.'

'That's right.'

Emma glanced across the room. 'That man is a constant surprise. We had no idea he knew the King. But he certainly looks more relaxed than I've ever seen him.' There was a pause. 'You're obviously very good for him, Bianca.'

Bianca wanted to beg the elegant blonde not to say things like that, because it sparked the kind of hope she wasn't supposed to be entertaining. Hope for a future which could never be hers, with a man who wanted different things.

As Xanthos walked back across the restaurant with Zac and his children, he couldn't seem to tear his gaze away from Bianca, who was sitting next to Emma and chatting easily to her—as if the two women had been friends for years. A sense of apprehension was rapidly building up inside him—yet another brick to add to his growing disquiet that here was a woman with the potential to destabilise him. He had watched the way she'd behaved with baby Eva—how her expression had grown tender and dreamy as she had cradled the little girl in her arms. That had been the clucky behaviour of a woman aware of her biological clock ticking—and whether or not that had been unconscious, he needed to heed the implicit warning in what he had seen. He had become so lost in her innocence, so bewitched by the wonder of her sexual awakening, that he had failed to look ahead. And he needed to.

They drank their tea and eventually rose to leave and, amid invitations to visit the Constantinides villa on Santorini any time they wanted a Greek vacation, he and Bianca returned to their suite.

'Oh, they're such a lovely family,' she said, breaking the silence which had fallen during the elevator ride to the top of the hotel.

'Yes,' he agreed steadily. 'They are.'

'Do you see much of them?'

'Not really. Our lives are very different now.'

But he could detect her sudden nervousness as they surveyed each other across the vastness of the luxurious suite, as if unsure of what to do next. Was that why she hurriedly walked over to the window, even though darkness had fallen?

'Oh, look—it's snowing,' she said.

He could hear the rush of relief in her voice, though whether that was because she was a lover of snow, or because it gave her something to talk about other than the thing they most definitely weren't talking about, he didn't know. But Xanthos knew he couldn't keep skating around the subject. Didn't he have enough unspoken stuff on his mind already, without adding even more to the heap?

'Bianca—'

She turned round and instantly he could sense that something had changed between them. Was it the tone of his voice which helped pave the way for that, or the way he let her name hang in the air—like a feather which was stubbornly refusing to float to the ground? Because suddenly he could see a different Bianca—a more brittle and watchful version of the woman who had given him her innocence. She was no longer the lover, eager to embrace her new-found sexuality. Her expression was cool and mildly questioning. He could imagine her adopting that look if she were dealing with a client in her lawyer's practice, perhaps twirling a pen in between her long fingers as she prepared to take notes. And if now he wanted to wipe away all her sudden froideur with the urgent press of his lips—he realised that to do so would be self-indulgent.

'I'm sorry,' he said heavily. 'But I can't give you what you want.'

'You can spare me the prepared speech, Xanthos.' Her voice was quiet but her dignified smile touched something buried deep in his heart.

'You don't know what I was going to say.'

'No, but I can probably guess. You were going to tell me there's no future in this thing between us—or something along those lines.' She shrugged. 'But that's okay, because to be honest—I agree.'

He frowned. 'You do?'

She gave him a frowning look, as if he were being either dense or disingenuous, and he felt himself resenting her cool logic.

'Of course I do. I'm not stupid. I may not be experienced with men but that doesn't mean I can't read the signs. What did you think I was going to do—pin you down for a date? Or demand that we start synchronising our diaries, even though I live in London and you live in New York?'

'I saw the way you were with Zac and Emma's children,' he growled. 'You want a family of your own one day—that much was obvious. You'd already told me that, but seeing you with Eva and Leo made me realise that carrying on would be crazy, because we want different things.'

'I know that…' she breathed, brushing her fingertips against the scarlet hem of her dress.

'And, just for the record, I wasn't expecting a relationship simply because you were the first man I had sex with. Believe it or not, I really am a modern woman—though, admittedly, a late starter. So why don't we just agree to part on the most amicable of terms and enjoy the memory of what happened?'

And for the first time in as long as he could remember, Xanthos was completely lost for words.

CHAPTER NINE

'So…' Rosie's voice was heavy with implication. 'Did Xanthos actually *say* anything?'

Bianca was trying very hard to hold back her mounting irritation—which was surely more to do with her own stupidity at having allowed herself to get involved with the Greek billionaire in the first place, than the fact that her younger sister was annoyingly trying to interrogate her.

'Of course he did,' she said calmly. 'Unless you think we spent the entire time in the mountain hut and then on subsequent flights in total silence?'

'That's not what I mean!' Rosie protested.

'Then perhaps you'd like to explain what you *do* mean!' Bianca knew she was being unreasonable but she couldn't seem to stop herself. It was as if her defensiveness had become a sturdy shield she could hide behind now that her bravado had started to slip away. 'I know you're a queen now, Rosie—but I'm not one of your loyal subjects who has learned to intuit your words before they've even left your mouth.'

'That's not fair, Bianca!'

'Then just say what you want to say, because I am time limited. Don't forget that most of us don't have a wealthy monarch to support us and still need to work for a living.'

'And that's not fair either!' Rosie's exasperated sigh echoed down the phone. 'You're hopeless when you're in this kind of mood, so why don't we change the subject? When are you coming out to Monterosso to see us?'

'Not any time soon,' said Bianca, before relenting a little. After all, it wasn't Rosie's fault she was hurting so much. The force of missing Xanthos had been like a sudden storm whose fierceness had taken her by surprise. And no matter how much she tried to reason that she barely knew him or to convince herself that she didn't really like him, it didn't seem to make the slightest bit of difference. Maybe their forced incarceration had provided an extra layer of intimacy. Or maybe the man to whom you so eagerly gave your virginity always occupied a special place in your heart. Yes, that must be it.

But she wasn't going to tell Rosie about Xanthos—about what they'd done or what they'd said—because if she shared her pain, it would only prolong it. She needed to draw a line under the whole affair and the best way to do that was to avoid going to Monterosso for the time being because, annoyingly, the place now reminded her of meeting Xanthos. Her voice softened. 'I'll try to get out in the spring if I can. Promise. But right now, I really do have stuff I need to do.'

But after she had terminated the call, Bianca didn't resume work immediately. She sat at her desk, staring at the calendar she insisted on hanging on her office wall every year, despite such things being considered old-fashioned. The January photo showed a clump of white snowdrops clustered around the trunk of a tree and although usually she adored the first flowers of the year, for once the scene looked as bleak as she felt inside.

She felt the wash of despair, wondering why she had allowed Xanthos to get so close and why she couldn't seem to get him out of her mind, no matter how hard she tried. Was it because the sex had been so incredible? Or because she'd enjoyed the unfamiliar experience of being part of a couple?

She thought about their matter-of-fact conversation late on Christmas afternoon, when she had calmly taken the initiative and told him there was no future for them. The truth was that her pride had wanted her to say it first—to signal the end before he did—because his growing distance from her had been obvious. But if her words had brought him relief, there had been surprise on his face, too—as if she had broken the mould. Did his lovers usually cling on to the bitter end? Probably. No wonder he was so arrogant.

She stared out at the dome of St Paul's cathedral, which dominated her particular patch of London skyline. It didn't matter *why* he seemed to have taken stubborn root inside her mind—all that mattered was the manner in which she dealt with the aftermath of their heady affair. She needed to move on. To start dating, like other women her age. To find a nice, steady man with whom to settle down and have a family. And perhaps Xanthos had been the catalyst she needed to put that in motion.

So what was she waiting for?

She downloaded the apps recommended by

her assistant and quickly learnt the rules of Internet dating, discovering never to agree to dinner on a first date, in case the man was so boring that you couldn't make your escape. But all the men seemed boring, even though in her heart Bianca knew they weren't. There was the hunky heart surgeon who invited her on a winter picnic in Hyde Park. The businessman who had rowed across the Atlantic with his brother and raised a shedload of money for charity in the process—and the fine art expert who took her to a private view at a groovy gallery where they could see lights twinkling all over Shoreditch.

The trouble was that none of them were Xanthos Antoniou and he was proving an impossible act to follow. Didn't matter how much she tried to reason that he wasn't the right man for her, deep in her heart Bianca wasn't convinced. It was like having tasted a morsel of rich, sweet chocolate then being told you would have to eat stale bread for the rest of your life.

And then one day in early spring, he rang.

His name flashed up on the screen because, naturally, they'd gone through the civilised motions of exchanging numbers before they'd parted. For a moment Bianca stared at it blankly, wondering if she was seeing things. She knew she should let it go to voicemail but suddenly she was sliding her thumb across the screen and praying that her voice sounded normal.

'Hello?'

'It's Xanthos.'

'I know.'

There was a pause. 'You don't sound overjoyed to hear from me.'

'How should I respond, Xanthos? Would you like me to burst into song?'

His low laugh did dangerous things to her blood pressure. 'How are you, Bianca?'

Oh, you know. Missing you. Obsessing about you. Trying not to view the past through rose-tinted spectacles or think about how it felt to have you deep inside my body.

'I'm fine!' she said brightly, looking at the wall calendar, which today was displaying the frilly yellow daffodils of March.

'What've you been up to?'

She saw no reason to lie, nor to be coy and *of course* she wasn't trying to make him jealous. 'I've been dating.'

There was silence.

'Xanthos? Are you still there?'

'Dating?'

'Yes. You know. Two hopefully single people meet in the hope of finding a mutual attraction.'

'And did you?'

'Not so far, no,' she said cheerfully. 'But I'm on several sites, so, by the law of averages, something should come up soon.'

'You're on a dating site?'

Wasn't it pathetic how that darkly dangerous note in his voice made her skin shimmer with pleasure? 'I am.'

'Are you out of your mind?' he exploded. 'You could end up spending the evening with a psychopath!'

Resisting the desire to make the very obvious retort, Bianca watched as a sparrow hopped onto the windowsill to peck at a crumb of bread from her lunchtime sandwich. 'Why not? Everybody does it.'

'I don't,' he growled.

No, of course he didn't. He just had to walk into a room and women started throwing themselves at him. Remember *that*. 'Was there a reason for this phone call, Xanthos?' she questioned.

There was another pause before he said the words she realised she was longing for him to say. 'I'm coming over to England next week and wondered if you'd care to have dinner with me.'

And although the logical side of her mind wanted to remind him that they'd both agreed this would be a bad idea and her aching heart was pleading for her not to canvass any more potential pain, she ignored them, using two careless words to seal her fate.

'Sure. When?'

He sent a car to pick her up from her Wimbledon apartment and was sitting waiting for her in a discreetly expensive restaurant situated on one of Mayfair's sumptuous streets. And although it registered in the back of Bianca's mind that the luxurious eatery was only a short hop to the Granchester, she made no comment as she slid into the seat opposite him. And if she'd been hoping—which she had—to have acquired some immunity to his powerful brand of sex appeal, then her hopes had gone unanswered.

He looked nothing short of spectacular in a dark suit and a pale shirt. His thick black hair was ruffled, his firm jaw shadowed, and the only negative she could find was that his eyes appeared tired. But it was none of her business what might have produced a fatigue which had the effect of making him appear a little battle-drawn and very, very sexy.

'Bianca,' he said, rising to his feet as she approached.

'Hello, Xanthos,' she said, but her heart was beating very fast and she knew she needed to protect herself if she didn't want to end up in bed with him.

But if she didn't want that, then why else was she here?

She was barely aware of the food they ordered and deliberately stuck to water in order to maintain a clear head and noticed he did the same. They chatted about his work, her work. The record New York snows and the latest political scandal in England. He made her laugh, and she reciprocated, and on every level it was the most enjoyable date she'd had for many weeks, by a mile. But it wasn't enough. Not with him. Because suddenly Bianca knew she didn't want this. She didn't want to skate over the surface and spend the evening making superficial conversation. She didn't want to second-guess his motives, or to push them away and ignore them. The question was whether she intended to be passive or proactive about her fate.

She put down her knife and fork. *Ask* him.

Stop playing games and just ask him. 'So why the sudden invitation to dinner, after radio silence for so long?'

Xanthos wondered what had taken her so long, because he'd been expecting this question a lot sooner. But he still took a heartbeat of a pause before he answered, because this was an admission which didn't come easily. 'I haven't been able to stop thinking about you,' he said simply, waiting for the inevitable response to his surprisingly honest statement and when she failed to deliver it, he raised his eyebrows. 'Have you been thinking about me, Bianca?'

She took several moments to fold her linen napkin into a neat square before looking up at him, her green eyes narrowed. 'Are we being honest?'

He felt a nerve tug at his temple. 'Of course.'

'Then, yes.' She shrugged. 'I would have to say that I have.'

'Internet dates proving a disappointment?' he mocked.

'Don't push it, Xanthos.' She folded her lips together. 'I'm perfectly aware that there's a perfectly logical reason for our mutual obsession.'

'Oh?'

'It's because we've undergone a traumatic and dramatic experience together, which means it's probably had a more profound effect than if we'd met in a cocktail bar.'

'And *that's* another thing I've missed about you,' he said in a low voice. 'Your intelligence and your judgment.'

She raised her eyebrows. 'Those are two things, actually—and I find that a very patronising thing to say.'

'How can it be, when I agree with you? Our near-death experience has left an aftermath which probably just needs to burn itself out. So let's burn it.' He reached across the table and took her hand, turning it over so that the palm was uppermost. 'If I were to ask you very nicely, would you stop dating other men and consider having an exclusive relationship with me?'

He saw her lips open and then shut again as if she were having trouble computing this and she pulled her hand away, as if his touch was only adding to her confusion. 'A transatlantic relationship, you mean?'

He frowned. 'Well, I have no intention of moving from New York and you certainly haven't said anything about leaving London.'

She pulled a face. 'Yes, I can see we really *are* being honest.'

'My boundaries haven't changed, Bianca. Have yours? I haven't suddenly transformed into the *nice* man you claim to want, who can commit to you long-term. If that's what you're expecting from me then I'll walk away right now, but if you're open to an exciting alternative, then…'

He let his words trail off but it took so long for her to answer that he thought she was going to turn him down and the prospect of that was something he didn't care to contemplate—and not just because of the unfamiliar impact it would have on his ego. But then he felt the deliberate brush of her knees against his underneath the table and suddenly her eyes were emerald-bright, her cheeks flushed as their gazes locked.

'Okay,' she said, her voice trembling a little. 'Why not?'

'Shall we go back to the hotel?'

'Or you could come back to mine? I know it's on the other side of the river, but Wimbledon isn't that far.'

He shook his head, thinking that perhaps, with his assistance, she could be persuaded to buy somewhere a little more central. 'I think neutral is better.'

He called for the bill and once they were alone in the back of his waiting car, she fell into his arms and they kissed like teenagers. He realised how much he had missed her as, instantly, he was aroused to an almost unbearable level of desire. With her sexual heat perfuming the air with its earthy tang, it was as much as he could do to resist the desire to touch her intimately and bring her pleasure with his fingers, as he had done once before. But he made himself resist, and of course that turned him on even more. As the car drew up outside the hotel, his blood was pulsing around his veins like hot lava and walking took a monumental effort as they made their way towards the private elevator.

'Oh,' she said, once they were delivered directly into a suite of monumental proportions and she went from room to room, examining the layout like a prospective buyer. 'This is different to the suite we had last time.'

He nodded as he hung up her coat in the hallway. The other booking had been last-minute while this was reputedly the best hotel room in London. But he hadn't booked it in order to impress her. It was more that he wanted to forget the past and live in the present.

But you could never really push away the past, could you? It still came back to haunt you when you least wanted it to.

'Do you know how many nights I've lain awake thinking about all the things I want to do to you, Bianca?' he groaned, as he pulled her into his arms. 'Was it the same for you?' And when she didn't answer, he placed his lips against her ear. 'Tell me,' he urged.

'Yes,' she blurted out unsteadily. 'Yes, I missed you.'

'Show me how much.'

But all she did was to tip her head back in silent submission so that he could kiss her again and he realised that this was a battle of minds as well as bodies, making the prospect of physical release all the more tantalising. She moaned his name as he stroked her curves through her closely fitting dress— her slurred incitement making his gut clench and his groin grow even harder. Every nerve ending in his body was aroused, as if she had torn off a layer of his skin and left him raw. Again he could scent her arousal perfuming the air—musky and provocative— and he picked her up and carried her into the bedroom, thinking how light and fragile she felt in his arms.

Her eyes were wide as he placed her in the centre of the bed and, without ceremony, he ran his fingertips up her leg until he had encountered the black stocking he knew he'd find there. Unable to sustain his teasing caress, he began pulling off her clothes with an urgency which only ever seemed to happen with her and suddenly she was doing the same. As if neither of them could bear to wait a minute longer. As if they had already waited too long. His throat dried and he felt as if he might explode. Because wasn't that how it felt? As if they had wasted too much time during these weeks apart?

He tried to claw back some of his habitual control, but, despite his best efforts to temper his reaction, he couldn't hold back his shudder of admiration as he reacquainted his gaze with her luscious curves and the rose-dark nipples which were crying out for the hungry plunder of his lips. Nor could he contain the sharp spear of lust which cut right through him, as he nudged the heavy tip of his erection against her moist folds and eased himself deep into her waiting wetness and she cried out even louder than she had done the first time he had entered her.

For most of the night he remained deep inside her, with sleep only arriving as the pale light of dawn filtered through the windows. The sun was high when she awoke and took him in her arms and the rest of the morning was lost in a haze of sensual abandon. The weekend spread out in front of them, awash with the bright sunshine of early spring, and while she was in the shower Xanthos had a toothbrush and fresh lingerie delivered to their suite, along with a pair of jeans he thought might fit her, with an accompanying cotton sweater.

'Clean clothes,' she observed when she emerged from the bathroom, before fixing him with a questioning look. 'Do you kit out all your lovers like this?'

'No. Normally, I would have sent you home in a car first thing and arranged to meet you later for dinner.'

'"Sent"?' she echoed, her tone acerbic. 'Like a package, you mean?'

'I prefer to think of it as creating a little necessary distance, because I'm someone who likes my own space. But since I'm only in town for two days, I find myself unwilling to waste a single second of my time with you.' And although she was still frowning, he brushed his mouth over hers in a kiss intended as much for manipulation as for pleasure and it had the desired effect as she whispered and wriggled and begged for more. Still he held back, enjoying a rare and heady sense of domination, until he could resist no more. And suddenly he was lost on a wave of something he didn't recognise. Suddenly, *he* was the one who was helpless, and the distribution of sexual power seemed far less one-sided than it had been before.

He tugged open her robe and tumbled them down on one of the wide leather sofas, choking out an urgent gasp of pleasure as he eased into her moist heat. And afterwards, when their breathing had lost a little of its ragged quality, he tilted her chin, his thumb stroking softly at her skin. 'Why don't you wander down to the hotel boutique?' he suggested carelessly. 'Pick up anything else you might need for the next couple of days and put it on my account. Anything you like.'

In his arms, she froze. 'Thanks, but no, thanks. I'm perfectly capable of paying for my own clothes, Xanthos. Why else do you think I've been working so hard all these years?'

He was unused to his generosity being refused, but the novelty value only added to her allure and, once she had sorted out her wardrobe to her satisfaction, he had the hotel arrange a dizzying selection of pursuits to occupy them for the next two days. The weekend culminated with an early dinner on Sunday evening, for he was due to fly out the next morning but despite the dazzling setting and Michelin-starred menu, they skipped dessert and went straight back to bed.

He was so hard. Over and over again he thrust into her—he didn't think it was possible to come that many times. Blitzed with satisfaction, he ran a fingertip over the curve of her hip, a sigh escaping from his lips. 'You really are the most incredible lover, you know.'

'I bet you say that to all the girls,' she mumbled drowsily.

He could easy have denied her accusation because he wasn't known for lavishing praise and most of his lovers complained about his detachment—a reasonable enough observation, but an irritating one all the same. Yet Bianca made him feel different. As if she had somehow peeled away his skin and imprinted herself on the flesh and bones beneath. Her body felt so soft and so pliant as she moulded herself against his that at times he was unsure where she began and he ended. Contentment stole over his skin like a silken snare and later he wondered if that had been the trigger which made him shatter the comfortable and easy silence.

'Did you tell your sister about us?' he asked suddenly.

Slowly, she raised her head, blinking long-lashed eyes at him as if confused. 'Well, up until a couple of days ago, there was no *us*, was there?'

'No. I guess not.'

She tilted her head back and yawned. 'Why do you ask?'

He shook his head. 'No reason.'

Bianca's eyelids felt heavy and the temptation to go to sleep was powerful, but something about Xanthos's tone was making her uneasy—because hadn't she been trained to search for nuance behind the stock phrases which people uttered every day? Up until this moment, her weekend with him had been perfect. Like one of those cheesy romcom films. She'd been on a total high. She'd even turned off her phone so the office couldn't get hold of her and she'd never done that before. But his stilted words made doubts begin to whisper into her mind.

She remembered her sister's question, asking whether Xanthos had *said anything*, and how she'd thought that a very strange question at the time. Half-forgotten fragments began to piece themselves together in her mind. Rosie's insistence that a complete stranger fly her home 'as a favour to Corso'. What had made her say something like that? She hadn't asked at the time because there hadn't been the opportunity and subsequent events made it seem as if it had happened so long ago. But something didn't add up and it was making her tense with apprehension—and coupled with that was the fear that this was all too good to be true. She pulled away from him.

'How did you say you knew Corso?'

There was a pause. He was still looking up at the ceiling. 'I told you. We have business interests in common.'

'Which struck me at the time as very vague. So that's all?'

This time the pause assumed the dimensions of a gulf and when he halted his study of the huge chandelier above their heads to face her, his black eyes were hooded. 'No. That's not all.'

She sat up, feeling her hair stream down over her bare shoulders, tempted to go to the bathroom to find a robe to cover up the nakedness which was suddenly making her feel vulnerable, but she didn't want to lose this moment in case it didn't come again.

Or that she might not have the courage to ask what she knew she needed to ask?

'What's going on here, Xanthos?' she questioned quietly. 'Why do I get the idea there's a bigger picture and I'm the only one who isn't allowed to know what it is?'

Xanthos's throat felt dust-dry. He wanted a drink of water. He wanted to rewind the clock. He wanted… His mouth twisted, because only fools thought that way. Hadn't he learned by now that wishing never got you anywhere? Meeting the wariness of her shadowed gaze, he knew he owed her the truth.

'You once asked me if my mother ever told me who my father was,' he said slowly. 'And I said no, she hadn't.'

'Only guess what? You've suddenly remembered that she did?' she suggested sarcastically.

'No, Bianca. She never told me. Somebody

else did.' He dragged in an unsteady breath. 'Corso, in fact.'

'But why would Corso…?'

He saw the exact moment when she worked it out for herself—faster than he would have anticipated, but then her perception and intelligence had never been in doubt. He saw the dawning of comprehension on a face still flushed with sex. And he saw something else, too—something he didn't want to acknowledge. Hurt, and anger, and disappointment— bitter seeds which would now flourish and destroy what little they'd had.

'Of course,' she breathed. 'Of *course*. It all makes sense now. Why didn't it occur to me sooner? I remember thinking you looked vaguely *familiar* when I first met you. And then there was my sister's ridiculous insistence that I travel with you, though I didn't stop to ask myself why. And you…'

She sprang out of bed and began scrambling around for her underwear and it was making a difficult situation practically unbearable to have to watch her slither into a tiny pair of black panties and matching bra. Like some taunting striptease in reverse.

'I understand it all now,' she breathed. 'You're Corso's brother, aren't you?'

'Half-brother.'

'Don't split hairs!' she hissed, bending down to slide on a stocking.

'You want to know what happened, Bianca? How it happened?'

'Not particularly. This is a story which has missed the deadline. It's too late, Xanthos.'

'Well, I'm going to tell you anyway,' he continued, as if she weren't smoothing sheer black silk over one creamy thigh and making his heart pound painfully in his chest. But more than the physical distraction of her beauty was the realisation that he *wanted* to tell her—and wasn't that dangerous? Because things always went deeper with her than with anyone else, didn't they? Somehow she had the ability to touch into a place which had always been out of bounds to anyone else. 'When my mother was about eighteen, she was brought over to the US from Greece and introduced to Corso's father, the late King, as a potential lover. They began a short affair in New York, for which she was paid—handsomely, I understand. Believe me, this was never a fairy-tale romance,' he added grimly. 'Apparently she had no idea he was married and certainly not that he was a royal, with the power to ghost her when she became pregnant with his child. Which is exactly what happened.'

'Don't you understand? I don't *care*!' she said, hunting around for the other stocking.

But Xanthos carried on regardless, making sentences out of the bizarre facts which had been torturing him ever since he'd discovered them. Saying out loud the words he'd kept hidden away in a place of shame ever since Corso had blurted out the whole incredible story. 'The money my mother had been paid quickly ran out,' he continued roughly. 'And her family back in Greece would have disowned her if she'd turned up pregnant out of wedlock, without even being able to name the father. So she met another man very rapidly and married him, convincing him that I was *his* child. I only discovered this when Corso came to New York to find me. It still feels pretty new and raw.'

She was shaking her head. 'But you're completely missing the point!' she raged. 'All the time you were having sex with me and supposedly being intimate with me—you were holding this back. Don't you see how it makes me feel?' she exploded, wriggling her soft cream dress over her curvy body. 'As if the rest of you are all part of some exclusive, privileged circle and I'm on the outside and don't count. It seems everybody knew about it except me.'

'Not everybody,' he contradicted. 'Corso knows. Your sister knows. Why would I tell you about something when I still hadn't come to terms with it myself?'

'I don't give a damn whether or not you've decided to embrace your precious royal roots. I can't believe my sister kept your identity secret from me!'

'But she didn't know we were involved, did she?' he pointed out.

'*Were* being the operative word,' she gritted out, before storming from the room.

He lay in that sex-rumpled bed, waiting to hear the slam of the door. But his assumption was wide of the mark because she returned almost immediately, wearing her coat, her face even more furious than before. Her eyes were two green splinters in her pinched face, her lips a tight line.

'I can't believe I've fallen into your arms again, or why I've just accepted whatever crumbs you were prepared to offer me. You couldn't wait to try to turn me into a convenient mistress, could you, Xanthos? Waiting until I was in the shower before buying me expensive lingerie.' Her mouth flattened in disgust. 'It's such a cliché!'

'I wanted to buy you something pretty.'

'I don't need you to do that—I can buy my own lingerie!' she protested fiercely, before sucking in an angry breath as if she'd suddenly thought of something else. 'Is that the real reason why you seduced me, despite your obvious reservations about me? So you could ask me all those questions about Corso, and find out what life was really like in Monterosso? Maybe you needed a few insider facts about the place where some of your ancestors came from, before you decided whether or not to make your association with them public. Was I just a convenient provider of information, Xanthos—who you decided to soften up by being physical?'

'You think I'd do something as underhand as that?' he demanded dangerously. 'That I would have sex with you in order to obtain information?'

'Oh, please. Spare me the righteous indignation. It's a little late to take the moral high ground. The bottom line is that you've misled me.'

But her fury couldn't disguise her hurt nor the clouding of disappointment in her beautiful green eyes and Xanthos felt the hard thud of guilt deep in his gut. 'Not deliberately,' he argued.

'You're splitting hairs. Again. Whichever way you want to look at it, I'd still call it a falsehood—'

'Bianca—'

But Bianca silenced him by lifting her hand, knowing his deception was only half the story. Because hadn't she been guilty of deceiving *herself*? Wouldn't that account for her disproportionate sense of hurt and disappointment, rather than the fact she'd been unaware her lover was a half-blood prince? Xanthos had made it perfectly clear this was never intended to be anything other than a casual fling. *She* had been the one to complicate it by reading too much into it—by wanting and dreaming and hoping. She had projected her wishes and her desires onto him, falsely imagining him to be the man she had been looking for. Was she going to imagine herself in love with every man she had sex with?

'I shouldn't be here,' she said quietly. 'I should never have agreed to have dinner with you. We're not right for each other. We never have been. Nothing has changed, Xanthos. *Nothing has changed.*'

And although the temptation to slam the door was powerful, she maintained her dignity by walking from that luxury suite with her head held high.

CHAPTER TEN

BIANCA SAT STRAIGHT-BACKED in the hard chair and faced the man on the other side of the desk who had caused something of a stir among the staff when he had arrived at her workplace a few minutes ago. Her heart gave another heavy beat of dread and there was nothing she could do about it. She thought about the last time she'd seen him, when she'd walked out of his suite at the Granchester, thinking they would never have to lay eyes on each other again. If only. She cleared her throat but didn't smile, because that would send out conflicting messages. Instead, her body grew tense as she picked her words with care.

'It was good of you to come and see me, Xanthos.'

'I was intrigued.' His black eyes were narrowed in question, his New York drawl a tantalising mixture of silk and gravel. 'How could I resist such a summons? I don't think an ex-lover has ever asked to see me in her *office* before. You aren't about to sue me, are you, Bianca?'

Bianca didn't react to the taunt, or the undeniable flirtation which flickered beneath it like a candle flame. Because she hadn't invited him here to flirt with him. She had asked him to come to her office because she wanted to be in total control of her environment—and herself—in light of what she was about to tell him.

She didn't know what his reaction was going to be, but at least she had her assistant sitting next door in case all hell broke loose. She didn't want the neutral space of a restaurant or a park, where their interaction could be observed by strangers. She wanted to be here in *her* space, surrounded by some of the things she'd worked so hard for, as if they would remind her of who she really was. Not the casual sexual partner of a deceitful billionaire, but an independent woman in her own right. Her legal qualification was hanging on the wall, alongside the wall calendar featuring the pinky-mauve sweet-peas which always bloomed in July. On the desk was a paperweight of a rare Monterossian shell, which her father had given her such a long time ago.

And in front of her sat Xanthos, hard and cool and utterly delicious. It was over three months since she'd seen him but not a day had passed when she hadn't thought about him—usually with a mixture of longing and regret. His black hair was shorter than she remembered but the virile shadowing of his jaw was the same. He wore an immaculate dark suit because he'd been in London on business, which was fortunate—if any aspect of this whole business could be described as *fortunate*. But she was grateful he hadn't been forced to travel thousands of miles just to hear what she was about to tell him.

The situation was bad enough—made worse by the fact that she had lost none of her susceptibility to him. The hot summer day meant she was wearing a new cotton shirt, which was already a little tight across her breasts. But now her nipples had started stinging uncomfortably, as if the only thing which could bring them relief would be to feel his tongue or his fingers working their way over them. And she didn't want to feel that way. She didn't want to be vulnerable to him in any way emotionally *or* physically.

She could see curiosity glinting from his black eyes as if this scenario was something he had expected all along—a change of heart from her perhaps, with the possibility of sex at the end of it. But there was wariness in his gaze, too—as if something was warning him not to take anything for granted. For one brief moment her heart went out to him, knowing that in a few seconds' time, his worst nightmare was going to come true.

'No, Xanthos,' she said. 'I'm not about to sue you.'

'Okay.' He leaned back in the chair, hands clasped together, two forefingers resting against the point of his chin as he looked at her. 'So why am I here, Bianca? Shoot.'

And because there was no way to soften the blow, the words came out more baldly than she'd intended. 'I'm pregnant.'

She watched as he grew still. There wasn't a flicker of reaction on his stony features and in a way that was worse than anger, or disbelief. As if his impassiveness drove home just how little he cared.

'I'm very sorry,' she continued, the dread inside her growing by the second as she recalled his determination never to have a family of his own. 'I know it's the last thing you wanted. It wasn't what I wanted either, but it's happened and I… I thought you had a right to know.'

He rose from the chair and for a moment Bianca wondered if he was just going to leave her office without another word. He was perfectly within his rights to do that, wasn't he? But he walked over to the window, startling the sparrow which had hopped onto the ledge for its daily donation from her lunchtime sandwich, the crumbs now dried out by the hot summer sun. The bird flew away and for a moment he watched its flapping progress as if he wanted to be gone as well. When he turned back the light was behind him, throwing his face into shadow and making his face impossible to read.

'You must be pleased,' he said. 'As I recall, you expressed a very real desire to have children.'

His words were as emotionless as his expression and Bianca couldn't deny a twist of pain as their coldness washed over her. But what else had she expected? Joy? Excitement? Surely she hadn't anticipated he would be-

have in the way would-be fathers were supposed to behave.

Get real, Bianca.

'You're not suggesting I *planned* this?'

'I have no idea,' he drawled, dark eyebrows
shooting upwards. 'Did you?'

'Please don't insult me!'

He nodded, as if her anger and indignation
were in some way reassuring. His gaze rested
upon her face. 'What do you intend to do?'

She supposed she should be glad he hadn't
asked who the father was, or demanded she
take some humiliating DNA test, but his
question still hurt. Suddenly her carefully
rehearsed speech was forgotten as she failed
to keep her voice calm, all the pent-up strain
of the past few weeks spilling out and making her voice crack.

'I'm k-keeping my baby, of course!'

'Good.'

The word took the wind right out of her
sails and she blinked at him in confusion,
before reminding herself that she didn't need
his approval. But that didn't prevent the sliver
of hope which shot through her, like sunlight
breaking through a dark cloud. 'I know you
never intended to be a father—'

'No, you're right, I didn't.' His words effectively killed off that brief flash of optimism. 'So what do you want from me, Bianca? Is it a wedding you're after?' He shrugged. 'As you know, I have never wanted to marry but if you're determined to legitimise the birth, I could probably be persuaded to put my signature on a certificate.'

She shook her head, hating the way he made her sound like some kind of amateur trophy hunter. 'I would never marry a man who didn't love me,' she said, in a low voice.

'Then that makes the decision very simple for both of us. Because I don't.'

Did she flinch? Was that why he continued with his discourse, still delivered in that strangely detached way?

'I admire you, Bianca. I like your intelligence and your humour.' He paused, his voice dipping by a fraction. 'And the chemistry between us is off the scale.'

'I certainly don't need any compensatory compliments from you!'

'Our relationship would probably have continued if I wasn't Corso's half-brother,' he continued thoughtfully. 'But it was never going to be for ever, was it? We both know that. Even so, I will support you financially.'

'I earn my own money,' she gritted out. 'I don't need yours.'

'But this isn't just about you and your independence, is it, Bianca?' he challenged softly. 'Not any more. I have no intention of stepping away from my responsibilities. I'm a wealthy man and now it seems I have something into which I can channel that wealth, other than my chosen charities. You can't prevent me from putting aside a sum which will one day benefit this child we have created.'

Bianca flinched. If only his last words hadn't fanned the flames of the longing which still flickered in her traitorous heart, a fact made worse by him choosing that precise moment to step forward, so that he was standing uncomfortably close to her chair. A shaft of sunlight had gilded his face, bleaching out the hard lines and inscrutable set of his lips, and as she thought of the little boy or girl who would one day inherit some of those features, a wave of sadness washed over her. She was filled with a sense of opportunities lost. Of something which might have been but now never would. Even so, she had to make certain. She needed to have exhausted all the avenues before she caved in to the inevitable. Prepared to put aside her own fierce desire for independence, she wanted to know that she had done all the right things by their baby. 'But you don't want to be a part of the child's life?'

'I think not. What child would ever want me as a parent?' he demanded bitterly. 'When I don't know how fatherhood works.'

'You could always learn,' she said hesitantly. 'People do.'

'But in order to do that, I would need to want to. And I don't. I'm sorry, Bianca. You know my story—surely you can understand my aversion to families?' His gaze bored into her—hard and cold as jet. 'I'm just trying to be honest with you. I won't make promises I can't keep because that wouldn't be fair to you, or the baby. You both deserve better than that.'

'But what if...?' Bianca clenched her hands, telling herself she was fighting for her baby but afterwards she wondered if she had been fighting for herself. For the tiny fragment of the dream which still remained. 'What if one day your child tries to seek you out and demands that you acknowledge your paternity? What then?'

Xanthos's eyes narrowed as her words took him to a future he had never intended. He pictured a scenario maybe eighteen years hence, when some unfamiliar and possibly resentful teenager might show up on his doorstep. Where would he be living then, in his chosen unmarried and childless state? Would he be an aging billionaire, still in his luxury penthouse in New York with a series of younger and younger girlfriends—a pattern he'd observed many times in his social circles? He felt a pulse flicker at his temple, for the image held no allure.

But neither did dealing with a newborn—taking an unknown leap into fatherhood and failing his child.

And he didn't do failure.

And what of his child's mother? Was he planning on failing her, as well? With Bianca it had always gone deeper than with anyone else. Somehow she had the ability to tap into a part of him which he'd always kept hidden from other women. But fundamentally, he remained the same damaged man he'd always been—and who would want someone like that in their life? Better she found happiness with the *nice, safe man* she'd told him she envisaged spending her life with, who could give her the deep and inclusive relationship she craved. Wouldn't the best thing he could do for Bianca Forrester be to walk away from her *and* their baby?

'Then I shall have to deal with whatever comes my way,' he said, feeling the vibration of his phone in the inside pocket of his jacket but for once choosing to ignore it. But his heart was pounding and his throat felt as dry as if he'd been running in a marathon, his unperturbed exterior belying the sudden unfamiliar emotions he could feel surging within him. He felt pain. Regret. And something else…something which remained indefinable.

Walking over to a side console, he poured himself a glass of water, raising his eyebrows at her in query, but she shook her head. He drank thirstily before putting his glass down, staring into a pair of wide green eyes which were filled with wariness.

From the moment he'd walked in here today, he had known there was something different about her. Something which hadn't been there before, which transcended the physical. A mixture of fragility and strength. Something soft and nurturing which lay beneath her cool and professional exterior. Xanthos had thought he'd known exactly what lay behind her unexpected request that he visit her office. He'd imagined that now she'd had time to reconsider her decision to end their affair, she would be regretting it—for whenever had a woman been willing to let him go? He had thought she might lock the door and seduce him. Her lying on the desk, perhaps— her crumpled panties on the floor—with him kissing quiet her shuddered little gasps. And yes, he couldn't deny that he would have been up for some of that because she had proved infuriatingly difficult to shift from his thoughts.

Yet the reality could not be more different, and neither could she. She wasn't dressed for seduction, in her crisp pink shirt and plain skirt, with her black hair piled on top of her head. It was difficult to believe she was carrying his child. He felt a twist of something unknown and intensely uncomfortable. Because children were the glue which bound families together and as far as he was concerned, families were toxic. His father's resentment had threatened to whittle away his self-worth, and his mother had chosen financial security over her only child.

Xanthos had buried the rejection as deeply as he could but now he started remembering how it had felt when his mother had cast him out. That out-of-body sensation of feeling completely alone in the world. Of realising he didn't have anyone to rely on. It had taken him quite a while to realise he could manage on his own—that he didn't actually *need* anyone else. And now, for the first time, he wondered how it had been for his mother. He had been so quick to condemn her. He'd never stopped to think that maybe she'd been hurting, too. And when Corso had burst into his life so suddenly, telling him about his real father—that had brought no relief either. How could it? His real father hadn't wanted him either, had he?

He forced his mind back to the present, seeing the way she was biting her lip. 'So what happens next?' he questioned slowly. 'Are you planning to tell Corso and your sister that I am the father of your child?'

'Why?' She jerked her head back, her brief show of anger unwittingly reminding him of her passion. 'Are you worried Corso's going to come after you with a shotgun, demanding you marry me?'

And despite the undoubted gravity of the situation, Xanthos felt the ghost of a smile haunting the edges of his lips. 'I don't think it works like that any more, Bianca,' he said gravely. 'And if it does, you can tell him quite honestly that an offer of marriage was made, and refused.'

'I would hardly call your disparaging question an "offer of marriage",' she snapped. 'You sounded like a condemned man being asked what he wanted for his last meal. And only someone who'd undergone a total brain bypass would elect to marry a man as cold-hearted as you, Xanthos Antoniou!'

She made him want to laugh. She made him want to kiss her. To unclip her glossy hair and feel those ebony waves trickle through his fingers. Even now he wanted her more than he had ever wanted any woman. But he mustn't allow himself to be distracted by the significance of her pregnancy. Nor her wit, or her beauty, or the pressing need of his own desire. And so he shrugged, as if her words had simply bounced off him like drops of rain, for many such accusations had been made against him in the past. Even if, for once, he suspected they had left their mark.

'Now we deal with practicalities,' he stated flatly. 'I suggest you send me your bank details so we can get those payments progressing.'

'And that's *it*?' she questioned, her voice

shaking with disbelief as he headed for the door. 'I send you my bank details?'

He reminded himself that he was doing this for her sake and their child's sake and that one day she would be grateful to him. But even so, it hurt to see the pain and reproach which were written in her eyes. 'What else is there to say? I am all the things you accuse me of and more. So go and find yourself a good man to marry to spend the rest of your life with, Bianca.' He gave a bitter smile. 'Because it will be a better life without me in it.'

CHAPTER ELEVEN

IT HAD BEEN trying to snow. The heavy clouds had been getting greyer and thicker all morning. Bianca stared out of the window to the street below as the first few flakes began to flutter down—fat and white and feathery. But the impending snow brought her no joy, no matter how perfectly timed it was to coincide with the festive period. In her current state, it represented nothing more than a health hazard.

Down there the world was super-charged with the anticipation of Christmas Eve, but up here it was strangely silent. She could see people scurrying towards their homes, laden with bags of gifts and shopping as they walked past shops which glittered with sparkly trees and bright lights. The air was buzzing with annual holiday cheer, but she wasn't really feeling it. How could she, when she was so heavy with child that she could barely waddle from room to room, let alone contemplate dragging decorations up the stairs to decorate her second-floor apartment? It had taken her the best part of ten minutes to put on a pair of boots, prior to braving the wintry elements to buy fresh fruit before everything shut down for the holiday.

She stared down at a woman pushing a buggy and found herself thinking, *In two weeks' time, that will be me.* It was hard to imagine herself with a baby. Hard to think that the precious life she had been nurturing would soon burst into the world. But she was trying to be positive and to count her blessings. She had done all the things pregnant women were supposed to do, while winding her caseload down as she prepared to take maternity leave. She had attended antenatal classes and taken gentle exercise. She had eaten all the best food, read all the recommended books, and her doctor had pronounced himself pleased with her progress.

Her mother and sister she had seen on only a handful of occasions and that had been deliberate. At least being thirty-eight weeks pregnant meant she'd had the perfect excuse to refuse an invitation to spend the holidays at the palace, accepting instead an invite to Christmas lunch tomorrow at the home of a very sweet couple she'd met at her antenatal class. She had wanted to distance herself from any well-meant family interference, determined to forge her own path going forward—as a single mother. It wasn't the life she had imagined, but who could honestly put their hands on their hearts and say that things had turned out exactly as they'd thought they would?

Despite the tentative queries which had come floating her way from Rosie and her mother, she hadn't revealed the identity of her baby's father. Not to anyone. And despite the obvious frustration of her family, that situation wasn't about to change—at least, not any time soon. Being pregnant had extracted a large enough toll on her already volatile emotions, without throwing the weight of other people's opinions into the mix. For years *she* had been the sensible one everyone had relied on and this was the first time she had ever stepped out of line. If people had chosen to benefit from her independent attitude in the past, surely she couldn't be criticised for it now.

She just couldn't face the fallout which would inevitably follow any disclosure about her baby's paternity, or get into some kind of blame game. Xanthos hadn't done something so very dreadful, had he? He had unintentionally made her pregnant— the type of 'accident' which had been happening to men and women since the beginning of time. He had grudgingly offered to marry her and, when she had turned him down, had set up a standing order, so that a generous wodge of money now came flooding into her bank account every month. At first Bianca had considered refusing it—sending it back maybe, or donating the money to charity. But second thoughts had made her decide against such a prideful action because what if she couldn't carry on working, for whatever reason? What if—and this was the most worrying question of all—what if she didn't actually *want* to go back to work after her maternity leave?

She heard the sound of the doorbell and inwardly cursed, because she wasn't expecting anyone. Living over a shop in the middle of Wimbledon village meant it was unlikely to be carol singers and her busy working life meant she'd never befriended enough people locally who might just 'call in'—especially on the busiest day of the year. Perhaps if she ignored the summons, they would go away. But then the doorbell rang again—more authoritatively this time, as if someone had just jammed their thumb on the buzzer and left it there.

A click of annoyance left her lips as she peered into the door camera, her knees sagging with shock when she saw who was ringing the bell. A man. A very tall and very recognisable man with the broadest shoulders she'd ever seen.

Xanthos.

Her heart was pounding so hard it hurt. She didn't have to let him in. She could pretend to be out. She didn't trust herself around him, not when she was feeling so strange and disorientated this close to the birth. But something told her he wouldn't give up that easily—and surely she wasn't nervous about seeing him, just because she looked the size of a small whale? She would hear what he had to say then send him on his way, wishing him a happy Christmas, even if the greeting got stuck in her throat along the way.

Laboriously, she made her way down two flights of stairs, leaning heavily on the rail, and was a little out of breath when she reached the ground floor and opened the door. But it wasn't the icy temperature which made her breath freeze and her skin start to prickle with goosebumps, because even though she had known it was him—nothing could have prepared her for the impact of seeing him again in the flesh, standing on her doorstep and looking as if he owned it. She saw a couple of female shoppers turn to look at him, their eyes widening with automatic pleasure, and for some reason this riled her.

Grateful for the support of the doorjamb, she stared into his face, but his carved features were stern and set—as if anticipating the flurry of objections she might be about to fling at him. But her throat was still dry and suddenly she was finding it very difficult to speak.

'What are you doing here?' she said at last.

'Hello, Bianca. It's good to see you too,' he replied steadily.

'I wasn't expecting you.' She studied him suspiciously. 'I would have preferred some sort of warning you were coming.'

'But wouldn't you have found some excuse to refuse if I had suggested it?'

'Who knows,' she said airily, 'what might have happened?'

His gaze flickered over her, those ebony eyes seeming to burn right into her flesh. 'I've tried ringing you. Several times, in fact, but you never pick up.'

'Usually, I'm busy,' she lied. 'But I always email you back, don't I?'

'Not always, no,' he growled. 'And even when you do, I find it a very unsatisfactory form of communication.'

It was also a very dangerous form of communication, Bianca had decided. It had an immediacy which created a false intimacy, which in turn had the power to fuel her foolish dreams. Once, she had been working at midnight when Xanthos's name had unexpectedly pinged into her email account. Infuriatingly, her heart had started racing but she had replied to his query about her general health with a few polite words.

I'm fine, thanks.

A reply had come winging straight back.

Why are you up so late?

I'm working. What's your excuse?

I'm about to go out to dinner. It's only eight p.m. in Barbados.

A red mist had entered her head and she'd been unable to stop herself from wondering why he was in Barbados and who he was having dinner with, all the while recognising that she had absolutely no right to indulge in something which felt uncomfortably like jealousy. That had been the moment when she'd accepted that casual emailing was not an option for two people with their history and she had been determined not to repeat it.

Was he recalling that conversation, as well? Was that the reason for the sudden frustration which had clouded his eyes, as if he wasn't used to having his overtures ignored, and which for some reason pleased her? It was certainly preferable to focussing on the flush of her cheeks as she remembered the way he could make her feel…as if her heart had grown wings and given her licence to fly.

And hadn't she been trying to forget all that soppy and meaningless stuff? Trying to get back to the person she'd been before she met him, by not thinking about Xanthos Antoniou at all.

But it was hard to forget that today was an anniversary, of sorts.

'So what *are* you doing here?' she questioned crisply. 'Doing a bit of last-minute Christmas shopping in south-west London?'

'Not a conversation for the doorstep, I think.' He lifted his dark eyebrows. 'So why don't you invite me inside, so that I can talk to you?'

It was a perfectly reasonable thing to say but Bianca recognised the danger of being swept along with his wishes by the sheer force of his personality. She told herself that allowing him to waltz back into her life—without any kind of warning—would be a dumb thing to do, just because she was feeling lonely and vulnerable. She forced herself to remember some of the things he'd said during their last awkward meeting. His heartless suggestion that she find herself another husband.

Remember how much that hurt, despite the bravado you displayed at the time.

Yet he was still the father of her child. She had agreed to allow him to provide for the baby whose life he didn't want to be part of, and wasn't an inevitable part of that equation that it gave him certain rights? Could she really turn him away, even though it was painful to acknowledge that it was exactly a year since she gave her virginity to him?

'Haven't we said everything which needs

saying?' she said, feeling some of her resolve slipping away.

We haven't even started, thought Xanthos grimly, but for once tempered his resolve, because deep down he knew he needed to take this at her speed, not his. Accommodating a woman's wishes ahead of his own was something novel to him and, although it cost him a considerable effort, he forced himself to slow down. 'All I want is a few minutes of your time.'

Their eyes met and he saw curiosity replace caution in her wide green gaze.

'I suppose you'd better come in,' she said grudgingly as she turned her back on him. 'Shut the door behind you.'

He followed her upstairs, noting that she was still as graceful as ever, despite being so much more cumbersome than usual. Once they reached her tiny sitting room he was able to look at her more closely and to drink in her sheer *magnificence* as she regarded him expectantly. Last time he'd seen her she had been dressed smartly for work—and back then the tug of cotton across her breasts had been the only sign she was carrying a little extra pregnancy weight.

But now…

Xanthos felt his gaze drawn irrevocably to her swollen belly.

Now she exemplified everything which was soft and warm and feminine.

The change in her was extraordinary. Like a ship in full sail, her huge bump was emphasised by a dress of pale green wool which fell to her knees, below which she was wearing a pair of black boots. Her hair was loose and even shinier than before, tumbling in dark waves over her slender shoulders.

He had known that this close to giving birth she would be large, but intellectual acknowledgement of a fact was very different from an emotional one, as he was fast discovering. Random thoughts began to pile into his mind and somehow he wasn't able to control them. He imagined his child's heart beating inside her and he felt…disorientated. And something else, too. Something which was gnawing away at his sophisticated veneer and leaving him raw and aching.

He shook his head. He had grown up surrounded by immense wealth, absorbing the often uptight behaviour of the class into which he had been born and recognising that emotional distance was preferable to the messy feelings he had observed in others. But all that composure seemed to have deserted him and as his gaze roved over Bianca's fecund shape he felt positively *primitive*. As if he would like nothing better than to throw his head back and roar like a lion, before picking her up and carrying her upstairs.

He took a moment to look around, his gaze taking in his surroundings with some bemusement. He didn't know what he had expected, but it hadn't been this. He was sending her a generous allowance. And her sister lived in a palace, didn't she? Had he thought there might be some trickle-down effect and his half-brother might have gifted his sister-in-law an enormous apartment? His mouth hardened. Maybe the offer had been made and that damned independent spirit of hers had made her refuse, just as she'd turned down his offer of marriage.

The room was compact, the furniture unremarkable and, unlike just about everywhere else, there was no sign of any festive decoration. No tree. No holly. No baubles. Nothing. He walked over to the window and looked outside. No garden either, just a street. He tried to imagine her here, with her baby.

His baby.

'Where is the...baby going to sleep?' he

questioned huskily, because it was the first time he had referred to his child out loud.

At these words her face softened and it was like the sun coming out—and never had Xanthos experienced such a powerful moment of bitter regret.

'Come and see for yourself.'

She led him into the smaller of two bedrooms and for a moment the breath left his lungs in a painful shudder because he was unprepared for the sight which greeted him, and the sudden answering thunder of his heart. A simple crib, above which hung a mobile of animals. The walls were washed a pale lemon, with a large and vibrant picture of a jungle dominating an entire wall. A room put together with love, not money. It made him think of all the things he'd never had. It made him think of Vargmali. A chair sat in one corner, with a small footstool beside it and even Xanthos, with his complete ignorance of small babies, recognised that this was where she might nurse their child. He swallowed.

'Who decorated this room?' he questioned thickly.

She looked taken aback. 'I did, of course.'

'You didn't think to get someone else to do it?'

'You don't think I'm capable of slapping on a few coats of paint, Xanthos?'

He thought of her halfway up a ladder, swaying precariously, and felt his body tighten. 'But you're pregnant.' And although he knew he shouldn't say it, he couldn't keep the words back. 'Why do you have to always be so stubbornly independent?'

'Because that's how I've always lived my life,' she answered.

She turned away and he followed her back into the sitting room, to stand by the fireplace. 'An empty grate,' he stated reflectively. 'What does that remind you of?'

Mostly to prevent tears from pricking at her eyes, Bianca glared at him. Either he was implying that her little apartment was reminiscent of a derelict mountain hut, or that he was feeling nostalgic—and both these options were as bad as each other. Didn't he realise that in her current volatile hormonal state she could be completely undone by a sentiment like that, even if it was patently fake? How *dared* he make it sound as if their snowy incarceration had been anything other than expedient? Was he playing with her see-sawing emotions in order to get what he wanted?

Which brought her back to her original question. What *did* he want?

A flood of dark possibilities rushed into her mind but one was uppermost. What if, during the months since she'd last seen him, he had met another woman and fallen in love with her, despite all his protestations that love was not for him? He might have changed. People did. And, unlike her, another woman might have softened him. Influenced him. Made him re-examine his beliefs. He and his new partner... She shuddered. His prospective *wife*, perhaps... What if they'd decided they wanted shared custody of his child and she would have no grounds to refuse, because what could she say?

I'm jealous. I don't want any other woman to have you or our baby.

But she couldn't do that. Not to him, who had already experienced so much hurt and rejection. And not to their baby either, who had a right to a relationship with their father. She could not and would not stand in his way, if that was what he wanted. She would do the right thing by their child—or else how could she possibly be a good mother?

Maybe she should have offered him tea, or coffee. If he'd called in anywhere else at this time of year he would probably have received a mince pie, but she didn't have any. In fact, she hadn't bought a single seasonal treat because Christmas had been the last thing on her mind. There had been too many other things to think of. Clothes and creams and unscented bubbles to put in the little baby bath which was wedged up against one of the walls in the bathroom.

She shifted from one foot to the other because her feet were starting to hurt, the boots digging into her swollen ankles. 'So go on, then,' she said encouragingly. 'Tell me what it is you came to tell me. I'm all ears.'

He didn't answer straight away and she wondered why. She had seen him looking all kinds of tense before. She'd witnessed the rush of adrenaline just before he'd made that emergency landing in the snow. She had seen delicious anticipation tightening his body just before a powerful orgasm shuddered through it, and she had seen the way he had grown so still when she'd announced he was going to be a father. But this was different.

'I've been thinking about our situation a lot, and I admit that in the past I may have made some poor decisions,' he said slowly. 'But there is still time to put it right.' His dark gaze grew shuttered. 'I want to marry you, Bianca.'

CHAPTER TWELVE

SHE WASN'T GOING to lie. There had been moments during the last year when Bianca had wondered what it would be like if Xanthos had actually *asked* her to marry him— rather than making it sound like something unsavoury which had been on *her* ambitious agenda. Those had been heady moments. Weak moments. Times of physical exhaustion and emotional stress brought about by a combination of long hours at the office, combined with her pregnancy, when she'd wondered what it might be like to have a big strong man to lean on, instead of having to do it all herself. But it hadn't taken long for common sense and her habitual independence to assert itself and remind her that she was fine on her own, just as she always had been. And right now she needed that common sense like never before.

'Gosh. This *is* unexpected,' she answered, with considerable understatement. 'A proposal of marriage, no less. What's brought about this sudden change of heart?'

'You're pregnant.'

'You don't say!' But as she waved a sardonic hand in front of her bump, a tiny heel suddenly scooted across the drum-tight surface of her belly.

Did he notice the fear and joy and vague discomfort which must have shown on her face as she felt the movement of their child? Was that why he suddenly moved forward to place his hand in the small of her back, gently propelling her into one of the chairs by the side of the fire which she never bothered to light because it seemed too much like hard work? She told herself that if she hadn't been so overwhelmed by everything that was happening, she might have stopped him. But then again, she might not. Because didn't it feel delicious to have Xanthos's fingers touching her like this—the sizzle of physical contact undeniably thrilling after so long apart?

And wasn't it wonderful to have somebody to lean on?

And then, even more disconcertingly, he

dropped to his knees and began unzipping her leather boots.

'What are you doing?' Bianca demanded hoarsely.

'I'm making you more comfortable.'

He must have noticed her shifting restlessly and correctly concluded that her boots were hurting. And her stupid pang of disappointment that he hadn't been bending down to produce a diamond ring was quickly superseded by the realisation that having someone remove her footwear in her current inhibited state, felt like the most caring thing which had ever happened to her. As well as spookily erotic. His thumb glided over her insole as he took off the second boot and the temptation to leave her foot resting in his palm and ask him to massage her toes was overwhelming, but somehow she resisted it and wriggled away from him.

'We've already had the marriage conversation,' she said, forcing herself to face facts instead of indulging in a fantasy which seemed to be getting more real by the second. 'You weren't a big fan of the institution, as I recall. In fact, you suggested I hunt around for someone else to be my husband. And nothing is any different since we had that rather difficult conversation—other than the shape of my body, of course.'

He went to stand by the mantelpiece, a study of power and poise, and although this meant Bianca was able to study him properly, it might have been better if she could have been spared that slow scrutiny. He had removed his snow-flecked overcoat to reveal a cashmere sweater in a cloud-coloured shade of pewter, which complemented his black hair and the olive-dark glow of his skin. His jeans were faded and moulded to his legs—as if they had been specially designed to emphasise his muscular thighs and the narrow jut of his hips.

He looked sexy.

He looked dangerous.

And, oh, how she wanted him. She hadn't thought it would be possible for such a heavily pregnant woman to feel sexual desire, but it seemed that was patently untrue. She thought about the way he'd removed her boots and how indecently good it had felt. About the nights when she lay awake, alone and scared and longing for someone to hold. No, not just *someone*. Him, and only him. Sometimes she dreamt of him kissing her. Touching her. Being deep inside her. And then she would wake up and realise it had all been a dream and a terrible sense of despair would run through her blood, no matter how many times she told herself that such a reaction was ridiculous.

She ran her tongue over the parched surface of her bottom lip, but her thoughts just wouldn't stop racing. Would it be so terrible to allow herself to wonder if a marriage between them could work?

'I think a lot is different,' he said quietly. 'But then, I've had a lot of time to think about it lately. I've spent the last couple of weeks in Monterosso, with Corso.'

She stared at him suspiciously. 'I thought you wanted nothing more to do with Monterosso, *or* your brother.'

'I thought so, too, but I was mistaken.'

'Gosh.' She couldn't resist the tart observation. 'You don't strike me as a man who would admit to that very often.'

He nodded his head in brief acknowledgement. 'You're absolutely right. I don't.'

'So what happened to change your mind?'

Xanthos stared at a photo of her on her sister's wedding day, enclosed in a golden frame, studded with emeralds. He thought how happy and smiling she looked—in contrast to the suspicious mask which Bianca wore today. Had he thought time and distance would have made her more amenable and she would instantly agree to his demands? Of course he had. But he had imagined that his own feelings on the subject would be as rational as they always were and he had been mistaken about that, too. The jolt of possession when he had first laid eyes on her today had been like a violent ambush on his senses and he had been unprepared for his reaction. The emotional fire which had raged through him when she'd opened the door to him was still burning, and he was uncertain how best to douse the flames.

She was looking at him expectantly and he realised that he would get nowhere unless he was honest with her. 'Suddenly, I wanted to know more about my half-brother. The only person in the world who shares my blood.' His gaze became hooded as he gazed at her. 'Apart from the child you carry in your belly.'

He saw the colour leach from her cheeks, as if she was unprepared for the emotional quality of his words.

'And my mother, of course,' he added suddenly.

She blinked. 'You've found your mother?'

'No, but I have someone looking for her. That relationship seemed to be something else in my life which needed to be untangled. To try to understand why she did what she did. And maybe to know how it affected her.' There was a pause. 'You suggested a while back it might be a good idea.'

She absorbed this piece of news in silence before responding. 'And did you tell Corso... did you tell him you're the father of my baby?'

'No, since it was obvious you didn't want them to know, and I respect your wishes. I suspect they've worked it out for themselves, Bianca,' he added wryly. 'But I neither confirmed nor denied the fact.'

'Go on,' she said, a little uncertainly. 'With your story.'

He stared down at the empty grate of the fire, before lifting his gaze once more. 'Spending time in Monterosso gave me a chance to evaluate my life. To examine things I don't usually care to look at. I told you early on that the man I believed to be my father had never liked me. It didn't occur to me at the time why his resentment should grow with every year that passed and why it should eventually turn into the kind of hatred which was hard to live with.' A bitter laugh resonated through him. 'It wasn't until many years later that I realised the physical differences between us must have been re-markable.' He shrugged. 'As a child you never really think about that kind of thing, but hind-sight gives you remarkable clarity. He was short and portly and I was not. By the age of twelve I was taller than him. And I was strong.'

'And insanely good-looking, I suppose,' she interjected, almost absently.

He raised his eyebrows but didn't com-ment, even though it warmed his blood to hear her praise. But his looks had never been in question, had they? She was simply stat-ing a fact. 'I can see now it must have been difficult for him,' he continued. 'People were always pointing out how little we resembled each other. I'm guessing that as his misgiv-ings grew, my mother's paranoia about being found out only increased. Long before he fi-nally demanded a DNA test, he began to take out his suspicions on me, in subtle yet cruel ways.'

'Did he...?' Her lovely green eyes darkened with distress. 'Did he hit you?'

He shook his head, for nobody had ever dared hit him. 'No, but there are many other ways to wound a child. Words are particularly effective. Tell a child often enough he is nothing and will amount to nothing and, sooner or later, he'll start to believe you. It was death by a thousand cuts,' he finished bleakly.

'Oh, Xanthos,' she said and the tenderness in her voice made his heart punch with something he didn't recognise.

'I didn't tell you this because I wanted your sympathy,' he ground out.

'Then *why* are you telling me?'

Unwilling to make any more pronouncements from the opposite side of the room, where he felt curiously exposed beneath that green shining gaze, he pulled over the vacant armchair and sat down so that he was facing her—so close that he could have reached out and touched her. And he badly wanted to touch her, for he had missed the warmth of her body against his. But not yet. Not until they had resolved this. *If* they could resolve this. 'At first I thought that giving you your freedom was the best thing for everyone,' he reflected sombrely. 'You had made no secret about wanting a family of your own. A proper family, in which you could be happy—the kind you'd known yourself, until your father had his accident.'

'But you didn't want that,' she reminded him slowly.

'No, I didn't. Which is why I gave you permission to marry someone else.'

Her short laugh was devoid of humour. 'Believe it or not, I don't actually need your permission to marry, Xanthos.'

'No, of course not.' He winced. 'Put it this way, then. I selflessly believed you might be able to find such happiness with another man.'

'Selflessly?' she prompted. 'Or selfishly?'

He ignored her challenge, just as he attempted to ignore the cushioned pinkness of her lips, as if that would prevent him from thinking about how much he wanted to kiss them. 'But that was before I realised the potential consequences of such an act.'

'You're not making any sense.'

'Hear me out,' he commanded softly, clasping his fingers together, as he sometimes did in the boardroom, when people were hanging on his every word. 'At the time of making that offer I was still reeling with the impact of discovering you were pregnant and I wasn't thinking straight.' He paused. 'But I am now.'

She stiffened—straightening her spine as

if unconsciously realising that she needed to pay extra attention to his next words. 'And?'

'And I got to thinking about the man you might one day marry.'

'Let me reassure you that there are no contenders in the offing,' she said, directing a flippant gesture towards her swollen belly. 'Looking like this doesn't exactly elevate me to the status of man magnet!'

'I thought about this unknown man bringing up my child as his own,' he reflected. 'Who might one day look at the strange cuckoo in his nest and start to resent him, just as happened to me.'

'But it's a completely different set of circumstances! My baby isn't going to be a secret to the man I marry!' she protested. 'He'll be going into it with his eyes open.'

'You don't think that biology—and nature—won't make a man naturally wary of a child which isn't his?' he demanded roughly. 'I'm sorry, Bianca—but I can't risk that happening. Once I suggested you might wish to marry me and you refused. But now I really must insist on it.' That hadn't come out exactly as he had intended it to and so he smiled, as if his smile would clinch the deal he was longing to make.

'Think about it and realise how heavily the pros outweigh the cons.'

She was staring at him as if waiting for him to deliver a punchline, but when one failed to arrive, she narrowed her eyes.

'The only thing I need to think about are the words you just used. You *insist* on it?' she verified.

'Perhaps I have expressed myself clumsily—'

'Another classic Antoniou understatement.'

'There are many reasons why a marriage between us would work, for we are compatible in many areas. You know we are. You have never bored me, not once—and that is unheard of. And then there is the insane physicality which exists between us.' His voice dipped. 'Believe me when I tell you that sex with you is the best I've ever had, Bianca.'

'And I imagine you've done some pretty extensive research in the field, so to speak?'

Hearing the bite of sarcasm, he held up his palms in silent supplication. 'I am trying to be honest with you, Bianca. I can be a father to our baby and a husband to you. We can create a family of our own and make it work. You know we can.'

She shook her head with what looked like

frustration. 'You just don't get it, do you?' she challenged. 'This has nothing to do with laying down the foundations for a good marriage and family life. That's not what's driving you at all, is it, Xanthos? Examine your motives carefully and you'll discover that your proposal is all about power, and possession. You're a highly successful man who's used to getting his own way and I've done the unthinkable and turned you down. Not only that, but you've suddenly woken up to the fact that I've got something of yours which is pretty rare. *Your child.* And while your response is predictable, it is also human nature.' She stared at him. 'You only want me and the baby because you can't have us. And it's a useless yearning—because the moment you get what you think you can't have, you won't want it any more.'

Her logic and her intellect drew from him a powerful sense of appreciation, even though Xanthos could see that both were working against him. Had he thought this would be a walkover? Yes, and three times yes. His life might not always have been easy but women had been, falling into his arms with an eagerness which had sometimes felt predatory. But not Bianca Forrester. Despite their earlier passion and the very pregnant state which was a result of that passion, she was behaving with a maidenly primness which was only adding to her considerable allure.

'And that's it?'

'That's it,' she agreed firmly. 'And since there is nothing more to be said and this isn't how I envisaged spending the night before Christmas, I really would like you to go.'

CHAPTER THIRTEEN

THE SNOW WAS coming down thick and fast
as Xanthos stepped out onto the pavement.
Icy flakes flew into his mouth and coated his
lashes and cheeks with a thin white mantle.
He stared up at Bianca's window but there
was no sign of her watching him, no wave of
farewell, or even making sure he was safely
off the premises and heading towards his car.

His car was parked on the edge of the common, but he turned in the opposite direction
and began to walk past the windows of the
trendy village shops, decorated for Christmas
with their glitter and their lights, his thoughts
whirling as fast as the falling snow which was
making visibility so poor.

He couldn't believe what had just taken
place in his ex-lover's apartment. She had rejected his proposal of marriage as if it meant
nothing, her accusation ringing in his ears.

That his words had been all about power and possession and nothing else.

What had she expected?

His mouth hardened.

He knew damn well what she had expected—more than he was capable of giving her. She wanted him to delve deep inside himself and to open up his heart completely. A heart he had carefully protected from pain since as long as he could remember. Couldn't she be satisfied with what he'd given her already? His lips tightened. Perhaps he'd had a lucky escape after all.

So why did his shoulders suddenly feel as if they were carrying the weight of the world upon them—as if he had lost something very precious?

He saw a shop door open and something drew his footsteps towards it. Was it the sound of taped carols coming from within, or just his need to shelter from the inclement weather? With snowflakes dissolving on his face, he stepped inside, realising too late that it was a children's clothing store.

Among all the miniature elf outfits and sparkly fairy frocks with wings, he could see tiny cardigans of pale wool and unfamiliar smocked garments, embroidered with carrot-wielding rabbits. Would his baby ever wear clothes as impossibly small as this, he wondered, and would he ever be there to witness it? Pain and regret rose in his throat as the sound of a particularly poignant carol split the air with its heartbreakingly sweet melody, and he was reminded of that night in Vargmali, exactly a year ago, when the children had sung their hearts out to the people of the village. He remembered the wonder and joy on Bianca's face as she had gazed at all the simple festive greenery, professing it more beautiful than all the splendour at her sister's palace. Her eyes had been half closed while those beautiful songs had been sung in a language she hadn't recognised, but which she had loved all the same.

And then they had gone upstairs to that high-ceilinged and chilly room and she had given him the greatest gift of all. He swallowed. Her innocence. She had done so without preface or condition, and back in London she had melted just as eagerly into his arms. He had just taken from her, he realised. He had given nothing back.

Even when she had told him she was pregnant, she had done the honourable thing. She hadn't grabbed at marriage to a wealthy man as many women would have done, but had told him with quiet dignity that he could be as hands-on as he wanted. And he had thrown it all back in her face. He had told her he didn't want to be a father. To go and find a different life and a different father for their baby.

Even now…even *now* he had turned up with a heartless offer of marriage. Perhaps she had been right. Perhaps it *had* all been about power and possession. There had certainly been no mention of love, had there?

'Can I help you, sir?'

He turned to see a young woman looking up at him. She was wearing a wreath of golden tinsel like a crown on top of her blonde hair and a pair of earrings shaped like wreaths, which were intermittently flashing red and green.

'I want something for a baby,' he said abruptly.

'Boy or girl?'

'I don't know. It hasn't been born yet,' he admitted, and he didn't know if it was the brusque quality of his words or the sudden brightness of his eyes which made her expression grow soft, so that suddenly she looked much older than her years.

'Let me help you,' she said gently, and Xanthos nodded.

Minutes later, armed with his carefully wrapped package, he stepped out onto a pavement now coated white, the thick snow still swirling down as he began walking up the street to the shop the young girl had recommended.

Because he wasn't done yet.

When the ring came on the doorbell, Bianca was half expecting it. She knew it was Xanthos. It had to be Xanthos, and deep down she was praying it was. She had told him to go away, yes, but deep down she had wanted him to stay, though she hadn't dared ask herself why. Did he realise that and was that why he'd come back? Had he observed the conflict of interests which was waging a war inside her? Had he noticed that too, along with her aching feet?

This time she buzzed him in, having no appetite for another journey down two flights of stairs—but more than that, she was reluctant to open the door to him, afraid that the bright snowy light would reveal emotions in her eyes which might be better kept hidden.

When he walked into the sitting room the

snow was thick on his head—a bright contrast to the ebony of his black hair. But he seemed oblivious to it, or the fact that he was still wearing his overcoat as he walked towards her. Without thinking, she perched on the window seat, not trusting her legs to support her as she met the hard glitter of his gaze.

'I have been arrogant and foolish, Bianca,' he began, without preamble. 'A man unable to see what was right in front of him all along.'

She blinked up at him, not quite sure she'd heard him properly but forcing herself to stay silent and not to prompt, afraid of influencing his words with her choice of question.

'I keep thinking about that time when we were alone together in the mountain hut,' he continued, his voice heavy and low. 'About the things I confided in you. Things about my past and my upbringing. Not everything, no. Not then. But believe me when I tell you that I have never spoken so frankly to anyone, nor felt so secure in the knowledge that you would never betray my trust. Yet afterwards I chose to push that knowledge aside, because it was easier not to think about the things I'd said, or the reason I might have said them.'

She wanted to tell him not to look at her

like that, because it was making her breathless. 'Xanthos—'

But he silenced her plea with a shake of his head. 'For too long I have deluded myself,' he continued slowly. 'I refused to ask myself why everything with you goes deeper than anything I've had with anyone else. I have closed my mind and my heart to the reality of what was happening to me. I thought that if I returned to my carefully controlled world then the pain I was feeling would go away. But how can it ever go away when I miss you so much?'

'What are you saying?' she whispered, unable to bottle up the question any longer, terrified she would misinterpret what she prayed he was trying to say.

'I'm saying the words that I've never said before for fear of laying myself open to unnecessary pain. But I love you, Bianca, and I'll risk that pain. I want to be part of your life and our baby's life. I want us to be a family,' he concluded huskily, shrugging his shoulders with an unfamiliar awkwardness. 'A real family. For ever.'

Bianca wanted to seize on his words as if they were a lifeline but she was scared, too. She had spent the last few months pushing him away, mostly as an attempt to protect herself and maybe it had been the right thing to do at the time. But he was right. Protecting her heart came with a heavy price and she was no longer sure she was willing to pay it.

Yes, his first suggestion of marriage had been clumsy but she hadn't cut him any slack, had she? Nor taken into account his shock at being told he was going to be a father. Essentially her reaction had been about her own pride and her own ego, rather than daring to acknowledge that he might be offering her an olive branch.

And wasn't she discounting all the amazing things he had done since he'd blazed his way into her life with such elemental force? He had crash-landed a plane and kept her safe. He had shown her physical love and ridiculous generosity, and now he had turned up covered in snow and opened up his heart to her, without restraint. Wasn't it time she opened up hers, to him?

'I guess I've always used my independence as a kind of shield,' she admitted slowly. 'I watched my mother and sister go to pieces when they didn't have a man to support them and was determined that was never going to happen to me. I was never going to rely on anyone, especially a man.' She hesitated. 'But maybe sometimes it is okay to lean on someone else.'

'I want to be that man, Bianca. Let me be that man,' he urged softly. 'Lean on me.'

Her heart turned over and she wanted to cradle his face in her hands, but still she wasn't finished. 'I thought I knew what I wanted from a relationship. That if I defined the parameters, then I would be in control of it. That's why I only ever dated men who made me feel safe but never actually made me *feel* anything.' She gave a short laugh. 'And then I met you, who was everything I'd warned myself against. I thought our near-death experience and the accompanying danger were what made me become your lover in Vargmali. But it wasn't that. I didn't really have a choice. I could no more have resisted you that night, Xanthos, than I could have stopped the beating of my own heart.'

She could feel the unsteadiness of his hands as he reached out to pull her from the window seat into his arms and she locked hers around his neck and buried her face against his shoulder. She thought she could have stayed like that for ever, but he tilted her chin with his finger, his eyes blazing black fire as they captured her within their gaze.

'I want to spend the rest of my life with you,' he said simply. 'That's all.'

'That sounds like quite a lot to me.'

'So you'll marry me?'

'Yes, of course I'll marry you… Xanthos, what on earth are you *doing*?'

'Isn't it obvious?' He reached into the pocket of his overcoat to produce a small box containing a diamond ring of such brilliance that it dazzled as brightly as the snow outside her window, as he dropped to one knee. And although there was a touch of bemusement on his face—as though he couldn't quite believe what he was doing—a trace of sexy arrogance curved the edges of his lips. 'I saw that crestfallen look on your face earlier when I didn't propose—'

'I was *not* crestfallen.'

'Honey, you were.'

Bianca started laughing as he slid the ring onto her finger. 'Okay, maybe a little,' she admitted, leaning forward so that he could kiss her, but he shook his head with firm resolve.

'No, wait. I'm not finished yet.'

Still getting used to the heavy ring glinting on her finger, Bianca stared in bemusement as he pulled something else from another pocket—this time bigger than a ring box, but only slightly. A tiny package in silvery-white tissue paper, its shiny red bow a decorative nod to Christmas. Her fingers were fumbling as she opened it to find a minuscule pair of white baby booties nestling amid the tissue, and slowly she lifted her head.

'They were the tiniest thing for sale in the shop,' he explained, his voice growing gruff. 'And I just couldn't imagine a pair of feet that would ever be small enough to fit them.'

They were possibly the most beautiful words she had ever heard, and Bianca made no attempt to blink away the tears which had sprung to her eyes—but why would she, when she saw them mirrored in his own? And then he was kissing her. Kissing her as he'd never done before. His lips were brushing over hers with unashamed passion but there was tenderness, too. When she began to move restlessly in his arms, he carried into the bedroom and lay down beside her and stroked her for a long time, delighting and exploring this new shape of hers. Her swollen breasts and belly, and the soft thighs which quivered beneath the feathering of his touch. He pleasured her with his fingers and she came apart in his arms and

called out his name on a note of joy and wonder. With an unexpected burst of energy and
an agility which defied her bulky frame, she
pleasured him right back, and afterwards he
ran her a bath and told her to go and lie in it
and relax.

Obediently Bianca sank back into the warm
water, gazing with contentment at the massive
diamond which was winking at her through
the bubbles, and at one point she thought she
could hear the muffled sounds of voices and
footsteps coming up from the street below.

Warm and glowing, she slid on her robe
and walked into the sitting room, her footsteps slowing to a halt when she saw what
awaited her there. Had a fairy flown in and
waved a magic wand? She blinked in disbelief
as she looked around her. Her small sitting
room had been transformed. The fireplace
was bursting with the warm golden light of a
fire, which Xanthos must have lit, and there
was fragrant greenery everywhere. It fes-
tooned the hearth and curled over the edges of
the pictures. On the table was a holly wreath,
and at its centre glowed four tall red candles
which matched the brightness of the berries.
And there stood Xanthos, so darkly beauti-

ful, his expression one of intense satisfaction as he studied her reaction.

She turned to him in bemusement. 'But, *how*?'

'The girl in the baby shop pointed me towards the jeweller's and the florist. After I'd bought a ring for my future bride, I went to the latter and explained that I wanted an instant Christmas.'

'And you certainly got that. Oh, Xanthos, it's so…beautiful. It looks like the dining room in Vargmali.'

'That was my intention,' he affirmed softly.

She went straight into his arms and he pulled her close as they sat and gazed in admiration at the little Christmas he had created. Later still he made her cheese on toast, and she wondered how he managed to make such a simple task look so sexy, unable to prevent herself from marvelling at his ability to concoct such a delicious variation of the dish.

'Oh, come on, honey,' he chided her mockingly. 'I'm as independent as you are.'

Yes, he was. Yet Bianca recognised that their independent natures had become modified through love. Their individual self-reliance had blended into something equally strong, yet mutually compatible.

And because it was their first evening as an engaged couple they went to bed early, their lazy kissing suddenly interrupted by Bianca's abrupt gasp as she stared up at him with disbelief.

But Xanthos didn't need to see her clutching her belly to know what was happening. He told himself he needed to stay calm—and on the outside he was—but never before had he experienced such a helpless sense of terror as he listened to the instructions she was stumbling out to him. No emergency crash-landing could be more scary than this.

'It's early!' she wailed, when the midwife arrived and made it clear there wouldn't be time to get to the hospital, even if the roads weren't already choked with snow.

'Only two weeks. That's nothing,' said the midwife reassuringly. 'Now, can we ask dad to find some towels?'

Xanthos obeyed every command which came hurtling his way, acutely conscious of the pain and effort it took a woman to give birth. As the minutes passed, he wiped Bianca's brow and caressed the small of her back and told her she was beautiful. And when, on the first stroke of midnight, their baby was delivered, it was to the jubilant chiming of the Christmas bells.

'It's a girl!' said the midwife, cleaning the slippery infant with efficient hands before placing a tiny seeking mouth against Bianca's breast. 'You have a beautiful baby daughter.'

Unable to speak for the emotion which was building up inside him like a dam, Xanthos nodded as he bent to kiss first Bianca, and then their baby.

His baby.

His senses had never felt so raw. He was aware of the primitive tang of blood and sweat and tears. The sound of the Christmas bells, muffled by the falling snow. And here, in this room, his woman and his baby, surrounded by firelight and love.

It felt…

He swallowed.

It felt like home.

EPILOGUE

Three years later...

EVEN FROM THIS HEIGHT, the illuminations of the palace's giant Christmas tree could be seen. Rainbow light flooded in over the child's bed, bathing it in soft, kaleidoscopic colours, but little Noelle was fast asleep.

Bianca stared down at the tousled black curls of her daughter before realising that Xanthos was watching her from the opposite side of the bed and, automatically, her heart turned over with love and longing as she looked at him. It had been an exciting day. He had been out riding with his brother early that morning, while Noelle had played with her young cousin—two-year-old Bartolo Corso, Rosie's child and the heir to the throne of Monterosso. Not that you would have known he was a royal prince to see his older cousin bossing him around, thought Bianca fondly.

'She's so strong and so funny and so stubborn,' she said softly, brushing an ebony curl away from a plump cheek.

'Just like her mother,' murmured Xanthos.

'Or indeed, her father,' she countered softly.

His smile was tender. 'Let's leave her to sleep,' he said. 'She's got a big day ahead of her tomorrow.'

Bianca didn't speak again until they were back in their own lavish suite next door, which commanded a magnificent view of the palace courtyard. She could see snow falling outside the huge windows as she went into her husband's waiting arms, snuggling into the warmth of his chest and feeling the powerful beat of his heart. For all his doubts about his ability to be a good parent, he had turned out to be the best father in the world—endlessly kind and endlessly patient. What child could fail to thrive beneath the tide of love which flowed from him just as she herself had thrived? 'I can hardly believe she's going to be three tomorrow,' she said, and gave a happy sigh. 'That was certainly a Christmas Day to remember.'

'It certainly was.'

'You were brilliant that night, Xanthos.'

'You were even more brilliant, honey. But right now I'm thinking of another anniversary which deserves celebration.' His voice was silky as he captured her face in his palm so he could look at her properly, and even in this muted light she could see the passionate gleam in his eyes. 'An occasion almost exactly four years ago, when we lay together in that bed in Vargmali and you blew my mind with your passion and your innocence.'

Bianca gave a sigh of contentment. So much had happened since that blissful night in Kopshtell. After Noelle's dramatic Christmas Day birth on the floor of Bianca's apartment, Xanthos had bought a large and quirky house overlooking Wimbledon Common, with a wonderful garden at the back. She had thought he might want them to split their time between London and New York, but he hadn't wanted that at all. Because family and home had become just as important to him as they were to her. The nature of his business meant he could just as easily operate out of England, which meant that Bianca had been able to go back to work at her old firm, once Noelle was a year old.

Xanthos had told her he didn't miss his

life in New York and that all he wanted and needed was wherever she and his daughter were. So they had married in Wimbledon village, in a beautiful church of grey stone with clear, bright light flooding through the stained-glass windows. It had been a small wedding with just Corso and Rosie as witnesses, her sister holding a squirming Noelle. She and Xanthos had taken their baby to Vargmali for their honeymoon, fulfilling her promise to Ellen—and something told Bianca that they would never stop visiting the place where their love had begun.

The two brothers had made their peace and, as he acknowledged on one of their frequent visits, Xanthos had grown to love the Mediterranean kingdom with a quiet passion which had surprised him. It had been that love which had prompted him to make a charitable donation to the children's hospital in Monterosso's capital, for research into childhood disease. And although before that Corso had offered him the prestigious Dukedom of Esmelagu, Xanthos had refused. Mainly because his beloved wife had no desire to take part in the cloistered world of palaces and crowns. But he felt exactly the same. He didn't need a title. He didn't need any public acknowledgement of his royal connection to the King of Monterosso. Essentially, he had always been a private man and he intended to stay that way.

The only sadness in their lives had been the discovery that Xanthos's mother had died in her native Greece, almost a decade previously. But a professional investigator had tracked down an aunt, and they were planning to visit her in the springtime—on their way to Zac and Emma's villa in Santorini.

Sometimes Bianca couldn't believe how perfect their life was. She had longed for a family of her own but had never been certain it would happen—for it had been nothing but a faceless dream. But now the faces had been coloured in and she could see them quite clearly. Xanthos and Noelle, and very soon a baby brother or sister to join their darling daughter.

'Happy?' questioned Xanthos.

'Are you?'

'More than you will ever know,' he said, his voice reflective.

He led her over to the window where they looked out at the palace courtyard. At the snow-covered grounds, which looked magical in the silvery brightness of the moon. But all the beauty of the external world didn't hold a candle to the beauty of the man who stood before her. She rose on tiptoe to brush her lips over his and felt the wildfire response of the sexual desire which had always flamed between them. His hands reached down to mould the shape of her bottom through her silky dress and to draw her towards him, as if to impress upon her the hard heat of his body, before lifting her up and carrying her over to the bed.

'Have we…have we got time before to-night's formal dinner?' she questioned breathlessly, as he began to slither her panties down with a speed which thrilled her.

'That depends on how many times I make you come,' he growled, and she gave a little gurgle of hunger as she fumbled for the buttons of his shirt.

And then he was inside her, filling her completely—heart and body and soul—taking her soaring to that place of total satisfaction. It was only afterwards, when they'd showered and dressed and she hoped the flush of her cheeks had quietened down before they presented themselves at the royal banquet, that Xanthos pulled her into his arms again.

'You still haven't answered my question,'

he murmured, smoothing her newly brushed hair away from her face.

It was a question which didn't require an answer— they both knew that. But she gave it anyway, because she liked to remind herself how lucky she was.

'Hand on heart,' she said, placing his palm over her breast, 'I never thought I could be this happy. And there's something else, Xanthos. Something I was going to tell you tomorrow, but I don't think I can wait that long.' She paused, savouring every second. 'I'm pregnant.'

Xanthos stared deep into her eyes. Once before she had said these words and his reaction had been nothing more than lukewarm, but in the intervening years he had learnt to accept his emotions. More than that—to embrace and to revel in them. From the very beginning he had felt differently towards her than he had towards any other woman. He remembered his fierce need to protect her when their plane had crashed. After that had come his admiration and respect and eventually his love, which had just grown and grown. He thought about their beloved child and the new life which was growing inside her.

Hadn't there been moments when he'd been

so full of joy as a result of everything she'd given him that he'd wanted to throw his head back and roar like a lion?

He smiled, then laughed.

Because this, he realised, was his moment.

* * * * *

If you were caught up in the magic of Her Christmas Baby Confession*, then make sure to catch-up on the first instalment in the Secrets of the Monterosso Throne duet,* Stolen Nights with the King! *And why not also dive into these other stories by Sharon Kendrick?*

Cinderella's Christmas Secret
One Night Before the Royal Wedding
Secrets of Cinderella's Awakening
Confessions of His Christmas Housekeeper
Penniless and Pregnant in Paradise

Available now!